the

A.

R.

E.

X.

project

Angelo Facchin

iUniverse, Inc.
Bloomington

The A. Rex. Project
Transformation

*This is a work of fiction. All of the characters, names, incidents,
organizations, and dialogue in this novel are either the products
of the author's imagination or are used fictitiously.*

iUniverse books may be ordered through booksellers or by contacting:

*iUniverse
1663 Liberty Drive
Bloomington, IN 47403
www.iuniverse.com
1-800-Authors (1-800-288-4677)*

*ISBN: 978-1-4620-1290-9 (sc)
ISBN: 978-1-4620-1292-3 (e)
ISBN: 978-1-4620-1291-6 (dj)*

Library of Congress Control Number: 2011916267

Printed in the United States of America

iUniverse rev. date: 9/19/2011

ACKNOWLEDGMENTS

The Beginning

During the summer of 2008, around the time of my 18th birthday, I started working on a book, with the idea of hoping I could one day get something published. All I had were ideas for a story and some 32-page notebooks. I started writing, and found that I enjoyed doing it. The start of the story was hard to find: I ripped and replaced half the notebook before I got it right. Before I knew it, a month later, I had finished the first notebook. By the time I finished the third part, I wanted to go further in the story. There are now six parts to the story and the one idea has turned into something incredibly complex.

The Inspiration

I am a die-hard fan of movies, comic books, novels, and video games. I was inspired one day, as I played the video game *Spiderman: Friend or Foe*. The Lizard, who had almost always been portrayed as a violent and savage being, was suddenly a smart, kind, and heroic individual, much like the Lizard's alter ego, Dr. Curt Connors. It always bothered me that Dr. Connors and the Lizard were two very different people inhabiting the same body. Unless one was suffering from a form of dementia, that shouldn't be the case. I started writing with the idea that I would be rewriting the story of the Lizard for me and my brothers, but the story became about someone completely different.

The story of Arex does involve an anthropomorphic reptile, but one who doesn't have a split personality, nor is living in a world where superpowers and aliens are commonplace. I also set the story in the past, not the future, like most comic books would be. The story did have to take place in a society very similar to our own, so I set the main story about a year after the first successful cloning. Please note that I purposefully left the formula for the A.R.EX. Soldier to be ambiguous, so that an explanation can be given in a later part.

This story is set in nine parts. It follows Arex and his acquaintances throughout their discovery of who he is, what he is, and his life in a realistic, real-world setting.

Thanks

This simple word is what I would like to say to my mother, who always believed in me. I would also like to thank my Nonna (grandmother) who would always support me in my endeavors. A special thanks goes to my English teachers, and to Nikolai Ronalds, who opened a door for me not to give up on my dreams, because this project was shelved for a year and a half. I would especially like to thank my uncle, Louie, for being my biggest inspiration in my life.

PART I

Transformation

1

"When you're creating a world, part of what you do is whimsy, part of what you do is for plot movement, part you do just for your own personal interests and psychological eccentricities…"

- George Lucas

Chapter 1

Flowing water and chirping crickets were the only sounds to be heard for miles around. The night air was warm, heavy, and incredibly moist. Even though the air was cooler than it would have been during the day, Emilio Perez would have still preferred to have the sun shining on his face. Yes, he knew the Amazon River well ever since he began his training to become a tour guide, but his job was made so much harder seeing as he didn't even have a flashlight with him. He knew it was never a good idea to stumble around in the night, escorting a complete stranger to a remote location deep in the rainforest. It probably wasn't a good idea to be doing something like that during the day, now that he thought about it.

He still couldn't believe what had led to this night. He met this person only two days earlier and was immediately stuck in a deal with him whereas he would escort the man to a specific location on the Amazon River's northern bank for a substantial fee. The description of the destination was very vague, only a few details were given to him. He would guide the stranger to a clearing with four trees set in a diamond pattern around it. One of the trees, the one nearest the shore, would bear the symbol of a fluorescent lime-green epsilon... whatever that was.

Emilio was thankful to be leading the way on one of those rare nights where the sky was clear over the rainforest. It allowed him to still have a modicum of clear vision from the moonlight. In his mind, he still had a lot of questions concerning the purpose of the escort, why they had to go to that clearing on that specific night, and why go there, in the middle of nowhere. Whatever objective the stranger had to achieve, Emilio wasn't sure why he was the one chosen and not his instructor, who clearly had much more experience than he did. There was this cold fear creeping over him, which told him something was clearly amiss. It was a sense of restlessness and paranoia that was all too familiar to him from his days as a security guard. Thankfully, his training had also taught him how to stay calm during situations like these. He was taught to resist any urge to talk to the man, to ask any questions that would bother his escort or make him angry. To the casual observer, it would have seemed that Emilio was gradually losing his mind. There was no way of knowing whether or not the stranger was armed because he wore a heavy, thick, dark trench coat. Emilio's instincts were screaming for him to be careful and that something terrible was going to happen. This overrode any kind of promise the stranger had made to pay him handsomely for the escort, and killed any hope Emilio might have had to gain some easy money for himself and his family.

The two arrived at the clearing and Emilio saw for the first time what an epsilon was. The fluorescent symbol glowed eerily in the dark like something out of those UFO sightings. It was shaped like an "E", but with rounded edges. What seemed strange to Emilio was the fact that no one was there to greet them when they arrived. His escort then took the lead and told him to wait near the riverbed for around 15 minutes before he would take them back out of the rainforest.

Emilio sat on a boulder, while he waited. There was still nobody to be seen for miles on end, not that Emilio could see that far. There was indication that something was happening when the epsilon started to flash in a slow pattern. It was mesmerizing...for a good two minutes before he got sick of it. He put his hands on his eyes, rubbed them, and then tried his best not to look at the flashing green sign. He slowly started to edge himself toward the clearing, hoping to obtain some sort of answer as to why they were there. He crouched down behind a bush to avoid being seen.

The stranger was in the middle of the clearing, pacing back and forth, occasionally glancing at his watch. He seemed just as impatient as Emilio for something to happen, or maybe even for someone to appear. Emilio looked at his own watch. It read 9:45 PM, and he guessed that they'd been there for around ten minutes. Emilio was ready to leave that location using the cover of darkness and abandon this foolish, seemingly rich, and suspicious stranger where he paced. There was nothing but wildlife surrounding them for dozens of miles in any direction, which would make tracking a fleeing person close to impossible. Emilio figured that there was no way that anything intelligent would be coming their way anytime soon. He could even forget about the money he was promised, which might never have existed in the first place.

Just as Emilio was preparing to get up and turn his back on the scene, a bright light suddenly appeared and started glowing where the stranger had been pacing just moments before. The man was now standing on the edge of the clearing, looking at the light, apparently satisfied that his patience had been rewarded. Emilio's eyes had to adjust to the sudden brightness. When they had, he couldn't believe what he was seeing.

The light had disappeared almost as soon as it had turned on, and a man appeared from what seemed to be out of thin air and had started to walk towards the stranger and started talking to him, or so it seemed. The apparition also wore a trench coat and had a suitcase which he handed over to his escort. In Emilio's mind there was only one explanation to the appearance of the other man: he had to be an alien from outer space. That harsh light had to be from a spaceship of some sort, and the strange symbol was a beacon for these ships to land.

It was an invasion, there was no doubt about it. Emilio's escape was more than ever a priority for him. He couldn't hear whatever was being said by the two men, nor did he care to know. He felt he had to warn the government, everyone, the entire world, of what he just saw.

He had just stood up and started to leave when suddenly, the two strangers saw him glowing thanks to the green epsilon, which was still glowing in the dead of night. Emilio saw the man point at him. He tried to run for his life, but was brought down quickly. His escort had just shot him in the back. His body fell to the ground as he struggled to try and catch a breath. As the shooter got closer, he unloaded another three bullets in Emilio's chest.

As blood started to pour from his mouth, Emilio saw the other man step next to him and look down on him. With his dying breath, Emilio saw the face of the man from another world...the face of a monster. Emilio's body wouldn't be found for months

Chapter 2

Saturday, April 4th, 1998, 2:45 PM
Henry's Law Firm, New York City

"We, the jury, find the defendant, Erickson Meyers, GUILTY of murder in the second degree of Brenda McEachern..."

Those words were still echoing in Janiece Ryder's mind. When she first heard them, her heart sank to her ankles. She still couldn't wrap her head around the fact that her client was convicted.

As far as she was concerned, Erickson Meyers was innocent. What little evidence there was against him, was purely circumstantial. Yes, he hated the victim and yes, he owned a 9 millimeter handgun, which was the kind of gun used in the murder. That didn't prove anything beyond a reasonable doubt.

On her way back to her office, she felt herself reliving the trial and trying to put everything together in a new perspective. It was a scenario she saw over and over again. As a defense attorney, her job description included being on the losing side of a case more often than not. In most cases, however, her client wasn't a provider, and was usually able to speak.

This case should have gone in Janiece's favor. The

circumstantial evidence didn't necessarily implicate Meyers, yet somehow it was allowed. The jury also quickly became biased towards her and her client. What made things worse was the judge rejecting Meyers' written alibi, claiming that not only he had confessed to the crime after his arrest, no one on the prosecution side had ever even heard of that statement.

It was bad enough losing that case, but losing to Kirk Hall was salt in the wound. Hall was not only one of her colleagues, but had the reputation for being a major-league kiss-ass outside of the office, an empty suit that personified nepotism in the office, and for being one of the most aggressive and ruthless attorneys to ever step foot inside a courtroom. Hall always did anything and everything he could just to give himself an edge over his opponent in the courtroom, and it didn't even matter who he was representing or who it was he was convicting. Janiece also found that in private, Hall was a racist snob who didn't hesitate to push her buttons just to annoy her. He often referred to her as a "glorified stenographer". Janiece was classified as an African-American female, which was the politically correct way to say "black woman".

Janiece was in a daze by the time she got back to the office. She knew that Hall wouldn't hesitate to stalk her, find her and tell her off, rubbing his ill-gotten victory in her face the first chance he got. She kept hoping that he would grow up and leave her alone.

No such luck today.

Hall popped his head through Janiece's office door. He had a wide grin on his face.

"Hello Ryder."

"Stop calling me that."

Janiece usually hated being referred to by her last name. It irritated her to know that people didn't want to use her first name simply because they deemed it unnaturally complicated. Of course, in Hall's case it was just another unnerving technique he used against her.

"You know, I'm surprised that you're still here. What are you now, 0 for 15 against me alone?"

"This isn't a game, KIRK. I care about the people I represent and not many times I win or lose. You, on the other hand, are playing with people's lives and playing dirty. It doesn't matter to you how many lives you destroy, just as long as you get the win. It's sick to know that I have to work in the same building with you."

"What can I say? I like winning. I find a way to win, and put myself on the winning side of things. Losing is not in my blood. If you don't like losing in court, then maybe you should have been a..."

"Don't you dare finish that sentence, Hall."

Janiece was sensitive about her singing talents and couldn't stand hearing them being made fun of. She loved to sing, and she was told she was good at it, but she felt she needed a more stable career, and singing wasn't her thing. She had always had a passion for justice, and decided she was going to make it as one of the few female African-American lawyers out there. She discovered, to her dismay, that racial discrimination was still very much present in American society. She really had no patience for people like Hall who treated her like nothing but a "glorified stenographer".

"It's a free country, Ryder. I can say whatever I want, whenever I want, and there is nothing you can do about it, but get uselessly angry at me. I'll tell you another thing while I'm at it: you better shape up and win a case, or Henry's gonna drop you like a bad habit."

"I'm pretty sure I'm not the one who needs shaping up in this office. I should have won this case because it was right for me to win this time. Working here really is a game for you if you honestly think that Meyers is, or ever was, anything but innocent."

"Alright. I'll answer that with a couple of questions: if your client didn't kill Brenda McEachern, who did? It was obviously a hate crime against Mrs. McEachern. She had laid Meyers off not that long ago. A hate crime. How many times do we have to see these? People just never learn to avoid the temptation of ending someone's life. Meyers hated Brenda for what she did to him."

"So did most of miss Brenda's acquaintances. She was a class-A bitch, everybody says so. All those people you brought at the stand said they would have done the same. And another thing: what happened to the copies of the doctor's report and written alibi?"

"I don't know what you're talking about.. The judge didn't either. I had to point that out. You can't try and pull a fast on me, Ryder."

"I'm not the one pulling fast ones here. You get everyone on your side just to play them like chess pieces that you think you can move around at will. Well I'm sick of being played. If you can say whatever you want, then so can I. I think that you're a sick, arrogant, immature little kiss..."

By then, half of the office had amassed around the doorway, waiting for the verbal carnage to ensue. The crowd featured Joseph Henry, their boss. He stood there, made sure that they both had his attention. He motioned for Janiece to head for his office and stay there.

* * *

Joseph Henry's office was located in the middle of the main corridor of the firm's floor. He preferred the middle to one of the corners because he didn't want to "isolate himself" from his staff and colleagues. Janiece sat down on one of the chairs facing Henry's office. She took some time to calm herself down. She soon felt really stupid for losing her temper the way she did and giving Hall the satisfaction of letting him feel superior to her.

Henry came five minutes later and closed the door behind him. Janiece felt her career in law grinding to a halt as her boss walked around her. Henry sat behind his desk and regarded Janiece. To her surprise, he wasn't scowling at her as much as he was smiling and even chuckling with good humor.

"That was quite the rant in that corridor. It's only one of the reasons why I like you so much. You have passion."

"Sir, I'm really sorry about what happened. I never should have exploded like that."

"Don't worry about it. I think that most people really enjoyed seeing you try and put Kirk in his place. What I don't like seeing is the kind of verbal abuse you take because of him. If only I were able to do something about this. If I had my way, I would never have hired him."

Everyone knew the story. Kirk Hall had just passed his BAR exam when a relative of his, a senator, had "recommended" him to Henry with the promise that he would work hard and be a good lawyer. There was also the promise of new furnishings and a brand new coat of paint for the building, which were both sorely needed. Unfortunately, it also meant that Henry couldn't fire him without a good reason and not suffer any severe consequences.

"You let your emotions get the better of you. That may be a fault, but I can tell your heart's in the right place. I'm sure that you had something on your mind other than your client's innocence."

"Meaning?"

"Meyers' case was different, not only because for the first time, you felt that your client was truly innocent, but it was also the first time your client was a single parent."

Erickson Meyers' son, Jason was about to turn eight. When his father was arrested, Jason was put into a sort of halfway foster house while the trial. It was no secret that Janiece had always wanted to have a family. At the moment, though, that seemed like a distant dream that could never come true. She always let her career come before any romantic relationship, so becoming a wife and mother was becoming impossible for her.

"Jason is in need of a family right now. He has no one left. I've seen the way Jason looks up to you and Rick seems to have faith in you. You have a big family, don't you? Jason needs that kind of environment to grow up in. You can let Jason know that you'll never give up, and that you'll be there for him. This is your chance to become a parent. The question I'm asking is: will you be a mother to Jason?"

Janiece thought about it for a while. She had always wanted a child of her own. She did have her doubts about committing herself to Jason. What if Jason decided he didn't like her that much? What if she proves to be ineffective and inattentive? How stable an environment could she really provide for Jason? What would happen to Jason if she refused? Finally, the answer came out of her mouth before she even thought about it.

"I'll do it. I accept. I want to be there for Jason, and take care of him. I just want his permission before I do anything else."

"Jason's at the first floor lobby with a social worker. She'll fill you in the paperwork you need to fill out."

She found Jason a few minutes later. It was astonishing how much he looked liked his father. If she didn't know any better she'd swear they were brothers. Jason frame, like his father's was tall and lanky, with brown hair and eyes.

She couldn't really figure out his demeanor, but she could guess by his bowed head that he knew all too well what was happening to him. His world had just come crashing down all around him and his future couldn't be more uncertain.

Janiece started to feel the pressure of trying to be a means of salvation for Jason.

Jason looked up and saw Janiece coming towards him.

"Hi Jason."

"Hi."

The social worker shook Janiece's hand. After a quick exchange of words she quickly excused herself to a corner, so as to not intrude. Janiece wasn't too sure how to start the conversation.

"How has the lady been treating you?"

"Okay, I guess," Jason replied, "but she kept telling me things like "It's not your fault", or "are you okay?"."

"Yeah, well, people feel the need to ask you these questions, so that you tell us how you feel."

"I guess you're right. I just want to go home."

"You can't, but I can go get your things for you, if you want."

"What do you mean?"

"What I mean is that I can go there, get your things, and take them back to my place."

Jason looked up to her. It was like realized what she was talking about.

"You want me to live with you? Really?"

"Yes. I may not be your real parent, but I would really like the chance to be a mother. I want to be there for you. I also hope that you'll still let me come around once I get your father out of jail."

"But everyone says…"

"Forget about what everyone else says. Just remember what I say. I say your dad is not a killer, and I promise I will do whatever I can to prove that."

With a hug to seal the deal, Janiece set about the task of becoming a temporary parent. A task that would prove daunting.

Chapter 3

Monday, July 27th, 1998, 1:15 PM
Operating Chamber

Several individuals were amassed within the dark confines of the operating chamber, making preparations for a test. It was to be the foundation of a new kind of weaponry and military reality.

Ever since the United Nations signed an international treaty practically banning nuclear weaponry from the face of the Earth, military organizations had to find new, creative, and often ludicrous methods of achieving their goals of overpowering their enemies. What these scientists were doing went beyond that, into the realm of the scientifically insane.

These people were lead by Patrick Sandlak. Also known as the "Chief", his vision for the world was particularly terrifying, even to his colleagues. He had discovered a formula that, he theorized, would create a weapon that would be highly efficient, deadly, and intimidating. After all, as his father once told him, intimidation is an essential force of nature.

It was a controversial undertaking for anyone to achieve, but it was original, and Sandlak promised it was going to change the world forever. It was a dangerous boast to be made, but the Chief enjoyed huge funding, a solid team to back him up, and a proven concept. Everybody on his team respected the Chief, but also feared him, for they knew he would stop at nothing to achieve his creation. Nobody else but him knew what ingredients were in his formula, and the thought of the end result would even make a high-ranking general shiver in fear. For the moment, though, his weapon still lacked a final test completion, something he hoped would come on this day.

In order to conduct the test, the Chief had found a suitable live subject. The weapon was to be tested and reviewed by himself and his colleagues. The scientists all felt they were facing an occurrence of the Third Kind. It certainly was an event to behold.

*   *   *

Outside the chamber, a small crowd had started to gather. The Chief's other colleagues, the ones not directly implicated in his plans, were waiting on any news from behind the metal doors. It seemed that the entire company had ground to a halt, and all people both inside and out of the chamber held their collective breath.

The crowd could hear muffled conversations going on, but they couldn't make out what was being said. The Chief had told them that the entire procedure would take about an hour and a half. The people waiting thought it was taking twice as long. They were anticipating the appearance of the Chief every second that was passing by. He would deliver the news of their success, or drop the failure bombshell that would end up demoralizing everyone for a few weeks.

The clock was showing 2:07, when there was sudden movement being heard from inside the chamber. The next thing the crowd heard was a piercing scream coming from behind the closed doors. Then, pandemonium erupted as metallic clanging and fearful yelling from panicked people was just barely audible from the outside. Panic ensued as the crowd outside scrambled to try and open the doors. In their struggle, the screams suddenly died out, causing even more concern and more urgent action. Finally, after five minutes and a call to emergency services, they were able to break down the door and break in the chamber. What they found, was a disaster scene.

An electric fire had broken out and the sprinkler system was struggling to fight it. The computers were caved in, destroyed, their wiring and boards exposed. Bodies were sprawled all over the floor with their blood being both charred and flooded. The test subject was still intact, but barely. It seemed unchanged, meaning that the weapon was clearly a failure on its first test. Nobody had any explanation for the paramedics as to what happened.

There were only three survivors in that room out of the dozen that were present when the test began. One of the survivors was Patrick Sandlak, his face badly scarred. The Chief's military vision had just hit a wall.

Chapter 4

Janiece Ryder had mixed feelings about becoming a parent, but she had to admit that there were improvements in her life so far. It felt good to know that there was someone waiting for her at home once she finished work every day. An added benefit of being a parent included a lessened work load. She was also growing to love Jason as she got to know him better, even though he wasn't really opening up to her all that well. She found herself enjoying doing things like watching TV with Jason, helping him with his homework, and cooking for the both of them. He was quiet, polite, albeit a little shy at times, knowing his situation though, she wasn't surprised. What did give a jolt was when he starting giving her that half-grin she had now gotten used to. It was Jason's way of trying to tell her that everything was fine, even when he clearly wasn't feeling too well.

She was hoping to be able to leave early, as she did everyday. She hoped as much, even though she didn't always have a family to go to. Her job always came first, and it was meant to stay that way, and so, it interfered with her hopes of ever having children of her own. She was a defense lawyer working under Joseph Henry's banner in New York city, which meant that she had to work hard. She also felt that she had something to prove in relation to her colleagues.

That was her mentality just two weeks ago. It already seemed like such a distant past. Nowadays, she had someone to come home to and actually take the time to cook dinner for. She had always wanted a family of her own and to be a mother to a child. Her work had put a damper on those dreams, because it took so much of her time. Her boss, Joe Henry, wasn't opposed to the adoption, and, in fact, he endorsed it completely, saying that it would be beneficial to her and to Jason once they grew closer to each other. And he was right.

The move allowed Jason to live in the same apartment complex as his best friend, which made Janiece all the more happier since she almost always worked past five o'clock. Even though Jason never had a hard time making friends, most of his classmates turned their backs on him because of his father's conviction. Kip Simon was the only one who stayed true to his friend, and Janiece was thankful that his parents seemed equally as understanding. She was comforted by the fact that she would always be able to find him at Kip Simon's. And if Jason ever needed anything while he was there, Kip's parents would always be there to help.

She was just finishing her lunch, a small baloney sandwich Jason had actually made her, when her office telephone rang. Jason was having difficulty dealing with his father being in jail. She expected the call to be from his principal saying that he was acting out in school. Instead of that, the caller I.D. showed as "D. CARTER".

"Janiece," came a voice from the receiver, "are you there?"

"Hi Daisy, long time no speak."

"And whose fault is that Ryder?"

Janiece couldn't help but laugh at that comment. Daisy

Carter was her best friend since they were ten. She was the only one Janiece allowed to call her by her last name, seeing as she usually hated being called "Ryder" just because they couldn't pronounce her first name right. Unfortunately, Janiece's work (and her new maternal responsibilities) also somehow meant alienating her friends and family.

"I really want to meet the little guy. I am officially going to invite you over to dinner next Saturday. That's four days from now, and I won't take no for an answer."

"Actually I didn't have anything planned for Saturday. I'm glad to accept your invitation. I'll see you at seven, okay?"

"That's the spirit, I knew you couldn't resist a chance to get away from both work and cooking."

"That's because I've got a friend who's looking after me, and my social health."

Janiece's thoughts were a little lighter for the rest of that day. Daisy never let things get too boring in anyone's life. She loved the fact that she had all the time in the world to make other people feel better.

"Speaking of health, how's your new protégé? I hear you are officially an adoptive mother."

"Yeah. I don't think I'm the ideal choice for this kid, though. I have more time to spare, but it might not be enough. I'm starting to wonder why I even decided to do this."

"So," Daisy said, "you're thinking of giving up, aren't you?"

"I never said that, I just think that he would be better off with someone who has all the time in the world. Someone like you."

"Not anymore. I've got a new job in a very interesting field of study. You're looking at a new member of the forensic team at BIOGENCORP."

"BIOGENCORP? I've never heard of it."

"It's in Albany, so I'm the one who will have the least time."

Janiece suddenly understood why Daisy was so urgent about seeing her as soon as possible.

"I get it now. I'll be there sometime before your first shift."

"Yeah, I'll talk to you later."

* * *

5:37 PM
Janiece Ryder's apartment, New York City

When Janiece got back home, she found Jason finishing his homework. He looked up and gave the small, half-hearted grin. Janiece took it as a warning to say that he had had a bad day.

She gave him as much of a smile as she could, knowing she couldn't really smile to him. They had an awkward relationship, which didn't suit Janiece, but also left her feeling helpless.

Jason wasn't telling her much of anything. She was still new at being a parent, but it was clear that he didn't want to tell her what was really on her mind. She never really knew how to react when she found Jason asleep at the kitchen table, using his father's case file as a pillow. He had snuck around that night and found it on her desk. She never found out why he had done that, or what he thought of that file. For now, all she could think of, was to give Jason enough time to heal his emotional wounds. She hoped to make him feel better before his father's next appeal, which was a week away.

"Jason?"

"Yeah?"

"A friend of mine invited us over for dinner on Saturday night, would you mind coming?"

"Okay. What's her name?"

Jason's father had told her that he never spoke much, in part due to him not being able to speak at all.

"Her name's Daisy Carter. She and her husband have been friends of mine for years. They're really nice people. I'm sure you'll like them."

"Sounds likes fun."

"AND don't forget that we're going to see your father on Sunday."

Jason lightened up immediately at the prospect of seeing his father for the first time in three weeks. He was in a much better mood for the rest of that night. Janiece was always able to keep her promises toward Jason, especially since she didn't make that many promises.

Chapter 5

Friday, October 23rd, 1998, 5:46PM
FBI New York City Office

FBI agent Mika Nomura was finishing a very busy week in her office. Looking at her desk, she had an urge to shred every single sheet of paper that was lying around and then burn the strips just to make her day. As much as she loved being a field agent, she hated all the paperwork that awaited her whenever she finished a case. As much as she also like her office, she hated coming to it. That only meant one of two things: Either she had just finished a case and had to write her reports and any other necessary paperwork she needed to finish, or she was coming because she about to begin investigation on a new case, which involved reading reports and research. Working in the field liberated her, though, in ways that made the tedious work worth the effort. She knew that crime was an entity that never has slept and never will sleep, so she wouldn't complain to anyone. At least not out loud, she wouldn't.

Her work also included undercover operations and interrogations that often lasted over four hours. Her superior, Corey Rodgers, was at the head of the Criminal Investigative Division in New York's FBI Headquarters. His load of cases sometimes exceeded the amount of agents that he had available, which meant his subordinates had more than his or her own fair share of cases during such times. When that would happen, Mika found out that her supervisor wasn't a pushover when it came to taking to the field himself. Still, he was often seen taking hard looks at resumes being sent to his office, probably hoping to find more decent, qualified help.

Mika was often partnered with Mike Scatchard, a rookie, who was a bit of an eager beaver. Mika found out that young Mike wasn't above accepting a mission on their behalf without consulting her, even tough she had four years seniority over him. She didn't mind their work load as much as she did her partner's attitude towards any case they took on. He was a little young for an agent, almost 24. To Mika, it looked like her partner had been dreaming of being an agent for all the right moral reasons and was now playing out a heroic childhood fantasy every chance he got. His enthusiasm for his job didn't deter his work ethic, but it did make him the annoying younger brother figure in her life.

As it turned out, Mike had said that he had a surprise for Mika when she got to the parking lot later on. Mika feared this because a "surprise" meant a brand new case for them to work on. With that in mind, she took her time finishing her paperwork just to make him wait and hopefully turn toward another agent for his next case idea.

*   *   *

Mike was leaning on Mika's car, waiting for her as she made her way to the underground parking lot. He flashed her a huge smile that had a glint of conspiracy behind it. It was that look he sometimes had in his eyes that she had come to know and dread.

In his hand, he held a brown envelope that seemed at least two inches thick. Mika sighed because she knew: the thicker the envelope, the more complex the mission, and the more work it would require, and the more paperwork that would need filling out.

"You're gonna love this next case I've got for us," said Mike.

"I bet you I won't. I'm too tired to even think about work," she replied.

"Oh yes you will, because this case just screams FBI agent Mika Nomura. It involves undercover work, most likely over an extended period of time, industrial reconnaissance, and possibly espionage, and no paperwork for the agent who has seniority."

Mike had just made it sound like it would be the ideal case for her. Still, she was tired. It was all too possible that she had misheard the part where Mike practically volunteered to fill out her paperwork for her.

"Am I dreaming? I hope this isn't a joke I swear Mike, if you're trying to trick me, I will make sure nobody finds your remains."

"No, I swear. While you're out undercover, I'll be doing all the tedious work. You won't have to lift a pencil unless your "new employer " tells you to. You are seriously lucky."

"What if I refuse?"

"Not this time, you have the experience. Chief said that it's you, or the case is gonna be dropped. He won't give this to anyone else, because you have a background in a specific field. Besides, I went out on a limb to get you out of the paperwork. I told the Chief that you were overworked and probably wouldn't want the assignment, so...I intervened."

Mika realized that her partner had gone out on a limb for her. She also realized that she was chosen for her extensive experience in the field of biological research. Her experience included a stint in a forensic research lab in Cleveland.

"When do I start?"

"Well, I suggest you get a good night's sleep and kiss your

husband tomorrow morning, cause when that happens, you will become a completely different person."

* * *

The next day, 2:53 PM
Albany, New York

The next day, Mike drove Mika to a job interview in what looked to be an office building in Albany. The building itself was very generic and looked like it was about 10 years old. The structure didn't even have a sign to indicate what company was located there. It really didn't seem so much different from the many other buildings she'd seen in her lifetime. It made her wonder if the company was even located there.

"THIS is supposed to be BIOGENCORP laboratories? How can anyone stand to work in a place where there is no way to tell your building from anyone else's? I thought that this company was supposed to be huge in their field."

"They are a small corporation in terms of office space and employee roster, but they have plenty of workload potential and they have an extensive reputation in the forensic science scene. Not only that, but their budget seems limitless, although suspicious. That's where you come in. As Sora Takahashi, you must infiltrate their roster and get whatever information you can on any wrongdoing."

"Can you be a little more specific before we go in there, please?"

"We really don't know, but there have been several transactions that can be described as questionable at best. BIOGENCORP executives have ordered at least a bundled dozen of every individual computer component from their specialized manufacturers. Every single component was custom ordered to certain specifications. The manufacturers have informed us that no software was ordered, so we think that BIOGENCORP have a group of tech people capable of programming the software they need to make their computers run. Not only that, some of these components are normally deemed incompatible with each other, since they're all different brands. Everything was taken from different companies, it's like BIOGENCORP's tech staff just puts Energy Star, Panasonic, Sony, and Microsoft all together in a blender and hit the Puree switch. The specific components include monitor pieces, motherboards sound and graphics chips, even the necessary screws to put everything together are custom-ordered. If they were a company like Macintosh or Microsoft, it would make sense, so here's the big question: Why is a research lab wasting time, money, and effort making its own computers when they can probably get a sweet deal on the latest technology all ready-made? Back twenty years ago, this wouldn't be a big deal, but these days, computers a little more widespread, and they cost less than the sum of their parts. Rodgers got suspicious and we put a warning flag on their receipts because BIOGENCORP already has their own network, and apparently their specific software, but now they are making the hardware to match? That would mean that they can't be hacked into unless it's done from the inside, because one would have to know the inner workings of their computers to understand what's going on. That basically means that the staff at BIOGENCORP have something big they wanna hide."

"I can understand how I fit in, but what will you be doing?"

"I'll be doing the tedious work. Rodgers thinks that I need to calm down and mature as an agent. Ten of BIOGENCORP's scientists have been reported missing recently. All of them within the same day. Ten scientists?! What are the odds of that happening? Either something happened while they were on the clock, or someone went after them for some reason.

Either way, these mysterious disappearances give us probable cause to investigate the company and anybody involved with them. We need you to get hired, so that you could access one of their computers and copy some software, obtaining any file that may seem suspicious and record anything that is out of place in a forensics research lab. On top of that, if you can figure out what happened to the missing scientists, and who exactly is responsible, that would be a huge plus, because their fates might be linked to some of that suspicious activity."

"Hopefully, they're still alive."

"One can only hope."

Mika found herself in a strange position. She knew that there were several risks, most of which she didn't care to find out the consequences to. What if she was discovered? What if there wasn't really anything to find? What if she couldn't find what was going on? How long would this case, this work drag on for? She always asked herself these questions, but she used to have a choice on whether or not to take a case. She had to explain to her husband that she had to go undercover and use an assumed name...again. He was worried for her safety, but he always admired her for her work. He understood that her job was to protect people and people from doing wrong. He always said "Okay" and hugged her tightly. Mika felt relieved to have a husband who was so understanding.

* * *

3:25 PM
BIOGENCORP Laboratories, Albany, New York

As they made their way inside the building, Mika was stopped at a checkpoint. She was wearing a basic and professional disguise, with her hair in a ponytail, and wore black specs instead of her usual contact lenses. She was given a "Visitor's

Pass" with a photo and her fake name on it. She was guided
to a hallway on the third floor. She was told to wait at a
receptionist's desk to her right. Mika got there and sat down
on a small wooden chair and waited, pretending to read a
novel.

She had been waiting there for almost five minutes
when she suddenly heard two men walking down the hall
towards her, engaged in an animated conversation. One man
was younger and taller and wore a grey business suit, and
had short, brown hair. The other man was slightly shorter,
older, wore a lab coat... and had recent claw marks across
his face. The scarred marks ran diagonally down from left
to right on his left cheek. It was very interesting to Mika,
because it seemed like those marks were very fresh and it
was very unlikely that he would have been working so soon
after whatever accident he was in, yet there he was. She also
wondered whether or not one of them was Mark Reeves, the
Human Resources executive she was to meet.

"Are you sure you want to perform a second test this
soon? I think you should rest some more.. or maybe drop the
project entirely," said the man in grey.

"You mean give it up? After only one test? We are counted
on to deliver on our promise. We have to go on with this
project, it's the future of our company... and I'm fine, thanks
for concern Mark," replied the other.

"You're ready to take such a big risk? Do you even realize
what would happen if you fail again? We could lose big on
this. And I don't mean just the exorbitant amount of money.
You could have been..."

"But I didn't so forget about it, okay? We are going to
finish what we started, And in doing so, we are going to
change the world forever, just you wait."

By then, they were about ten feet away from Mika and
they had spotted her. She looked up, "noticed" them, and put

her book in her purse. She took a stride to them and bowed slightly as is Japanese custom.

"Hello. Do you work here?"

"Yes," replied the scarred man, "can we help you with something?"

"My name is Sora Takashi. I am looking for Mark Reeves. I made an appointment for a job interview today."

Mika was very nervous and figured that her accent was showing. She was born and raised in Los Angeles and her accent involved making statements that sounded like she was asking a question. Her alter ego, Sora Takahashi, was from Cleveland, Ohio were she interned as a forensic scientist. She hoped that they didn't know that, or didn't notice.

"I'm Mark Reeves," said the man in the suit, "pleased to meet you miss Takahashi. Please come to my office and I will talk to you privately."

"Thank you."

* * *

They got inside Reeve's office and Mika was already disappointed by what she saw. There were no diplomas, no plants, and no photographs of office parties. The space looked pretty bland and devoid of any special personal attention. It reminded her of the set of an old science fiction film that looked a little too perfect and unrealistic. Mika wondered whether or not Reeves actually spent a lot of time in his own office.

"Please, sit down."

"Thank you."

Reeves pulled out a file and opened it. It contained all the information she had sent to him.

"Your resume is very impressive. I talked to your ex-employers. They praised your work ethic, in fact they wished you were still in Ohio. I can see that you'd be a great fit here."

"Thank You."

"Just one question, why would you leave such a stable job to come work here?"

"I'm getting married. Steve lives in Troy and I really want to find a career in this field. Working here is a good step, because it's a lot closer to home."

Reeves fell silent. His eyes were riveted on her resume. Something in it had caught his eye.

"You're...a certified signer?"

Mika had learned sign language at an early age, because her mother was deaf. She had put that skill on her resume just in case she had to work with someone who needed to communicate in that manner.

"I am. My mother was deaf. Why?"

"It just so happens that we have been looking for certified signer for a while now. We need someone who's able to communicate using sign language. Unfortunately, these people are few and far between. If you don't mind would you do a job for us before you start in the lab?"

"What would I need to do?"

"I need you to come with the colleague of mine you just saw me talking to. You both will be going to a prison, where a prisoner will be chosen to volunteer for a project we are conducting. We need you to translate his signing for us. I hope you're available in two days if it's not too much trouble."

"Actually, I am. Just give me the details, and I will be there."

Mika left the building with a mixed feeling. Not only was she chosen for lab work, but she was also picked for a special task. She also learned that something had happened with a very important project during a test. Whatever happened was so incredible it left a highly experienced scientist with some nasty-looking scars on his face. She had to take this job in order to be able to obtain all the details she could squeeze out of it, and leave her partner Mike with the task of writing a report on her behalf.

Chapter 6

Monday, October 26th, 1998, 1:34 PM
Bare Hill Correctional Facility,
Franklin County, New York

Mika was back in her simple disguise soon enough as she got into a limo with Patrick Sandlak. She found herself staring at Sandlak's scars, which made her a little uncomfortable. She decided to approach the subject, hoping to get some information as to what happened to him.

"I hope you don't mind... I would like to ask you how you got those scars on your face."

"I don't mind at all. You're the first one who's ever dared to ask me that. I'm guessing that, like many others, you feel a little uneasy looking at me, your eyes going straight to my cheek. It doesn't really bother me, so much as it makes me feel a little awkward in front of people. I went camping with my family about three months ago, when I was attacked by an angry bear, and I narrowly escaped with my life."

"An adult bear?"

"A Grizzly, yes."

Sandlak was lying, that much was clear. Mika knew that Sandlak's scars weren't made by a Grizzly bear, because they were much too thin and precise. Besides, Sandlak didn't have children and was never married. It was unclear to Mika why Sandlak would be lying to her, unless he had something to hide. He really took her for a fool, if he was going to give her that kind of story when he knew that the person he talking to had a bachelor's degree in forensic sciences.

"So, who is this person we're going to meet?"

"His name is Erickson Meyers."

"From the McEachern trial?"

"You've heard about it. How much do you know?"

"I know that Mr. Meyers is mute. He had his larynx damaged eight months ago. He was fired from his job a few days after he got back from the hospital simply because he would be unable to speak for the rest of his life. The prosecution stated that Meyers killed Lester McEachern in rage for being so biased against him and others that would be considered minorities. The case revolved around the idea that it was an anti-discrimination crime, which is why Meyers became a martyr in the public eye. No one ever had any real physical evidence against him, it was all circumstantial. Several witnesses stated that an individual that matched his description was seen near the scene of the crime. They basically said that a medium height, medium-built, Caucasian male with brown hair and eyes was walking down the street on the murder near the McEacherns' home. The case was full of holes, but the state got a conviction anyway and Meyers got 15 years for second-degree murder."

"You've got a great eye for details. You probably agree with me when I say this was clearly a case where the prosecution's goal was to find A culprit and not THE culprit. I hope to change Meyer's life for the better. The idea here is to get him out on bond and employ him in testing a new drug we've been trying to bring on the market. This is were you come in. You must translate what he signs for me once we meet him."

Mika was slowly getting more and more suspicious of Patrick Sandlak. Why would Sandlak be interested in a prisoner like Meyers? Unfortunately, research labs had a bit of a habit of employing convicted criminals as janitors or volunteers for testing, so this simply wasn't enough to put in a report and have criminal charges filed. All Mika had was a bunch of suspicious-looking receipts and a gut feeling. She had to be patient and wait for Sandlak and BIOGENCORP to show their true colors.

* * *

When they entered the penitentiary, they were escorted to the warden's office located just inside the building by armed guards. James Keith greeted them with a firm handshake and an even firmer frown.

"I've reviewed your papers and everything seems to be in order. Meyers' usually only gets his son and his attorney as visitors but I told him to expect you today."

"Thank you for letting us see him. We couldn't have hoped for a better volunteer."

"I hope you realize that he might not agree to be a part of your little experiment."

"That's why I came prepared to sweeten the deal for him."

They started down a long corridor with a door that lead to the main cell area. Mika had reviewed her signs to make sure that she didn't misunderstand anything Meyers "said". She was fairly confident of her abilities, but she hadn't used them in years ever since her mother died.

When they got to Meyers' cell, he immediately got up, but quickly sat down, disappointed that his visitors were probably not who he was expecting. James Keith had probably forgot to mention to him which visitors he was getting.

Erickson Meyers was unspectacular in terms of build. He was 5'11" with brown hair and eyes. He was lanky, with made him seem a little taller than he actually was. He looked sickly and frail, and the expression on his face showed months of constant disappointment and frustration. In his hand, he held a notebook in which he would write down everything he said.

Patrick Sandlak introduced himself and shook Meyers' hand. There wasn't much energy in Meyers as his hand flopped down on his knee, a sign that prison food wasn't agreeing with him.

"Hello Mr. Meyers, my name is Patrick Sandlak. I am a researcher at BIOGENCORP, a research company in Albany. We are currently working on an experimental drug that regenerates human tissue and organs. I am fully aware of your situation and hope to be able to help you. I think that you would be the perfect volunteer for testing this drug. My belief is that you're innocent and if this works, you will show the city of New York how wrong they were. I sincerely hope that we can count on your cooperation. We are prepared to compensate you for your time with us. Miss Takashi here will translate anything you say, so if you have any questions, please feel free to ask anything you want."

Sandlak finished with that and awaited Meyers' response. Meyers nodded to Mika and started to sign.

Mika immediately noticed that Meyers had little time to practice sign language. All he had was a book on the basics of sign on a small desk near his bed. Not only that, but Meyers was hesitant, often unable to make complete sentences and he made several mistakes which Mika had to correct for him. Meyers gave a simple enough statement.

"I would be glad to cooperate in your experiment, and hope it works as I have trouble communicating with people here. If the compensation you were referring to is monetary, I would like it if the money was given to my son, instead of me. I need to lighten miss Ryder's financial load any way I can."

The two visitors got inside their vehicle a few minutes

later, with a special penitentiary truck holding Meyers inside lagging not too far behind.

"At first, I was worried I was out of practice," said Mika, "but apparently there's worse. How could someone like Meyers, a complete amateur, be allowed to testify in his own defense? He must've been a nightmare to translate six months ago."

"He wasn't allowed to testify. A signer testified in court that Meyers had confessed to interrogators through sign, but he never took to the stand because he couldn't sign. The prosecution made sure of that. His lawyer, miss Ryder, had tried to present his written alibi to court only to have the prosecution file a motion to reject it, claiming they never received such information, and the judge. With his alibi gone and his being unable to speak for himself, his defense crumbled. It's sad, really."

That couldn't be right. How could this have happened? Meyers trial should never have ended with his conviction. She had to bring this information to Corey Rodger's attention as soon as she could.

*   *   *

3:15 PM
Rome, New York

Mika got back home soon after and immediately got in contact with Mike, her partner.

"I need you to have a look at the McEachern case from six months ago. The one who was convicted, his name is Rick Meyers. The case was full of holes, and for some reason, Patrick Sandlak just practically promised him that he would give him his voice back, and pay him handsomely with something. He's planning to use some sort of experimental drug on Meyers. I want to know about this lawyer of his, her name is Janiece Ryder. Also, take a look at Patrick Sandlak, I need to know his background. I need to know who they are, because Meyers has just been selected by Sandlak to be his guinea pig, and I don't think it's because he feels like helping someone get his voice back."

Chapter 7

Monday, October 26th, 1998, 3:23 PM
Bare Hill Correctional Facility

"What?!"

Janiece couldn't believe what she was hearing. Erickson Meyers was extradite from the facility by some scientist supposedly handing warden Keith a paper signed by her hand. Not only that, but it only happened two hours earlier! She expected Rick to be waiting in his cell for his son to visit him. Instead, he was gone, leaving Janiece to stare at a legal document she'd never seen with what looked very much like her own signature on it. It felt like the paper in her hands had slapped her in the face and then proceeded to give her the finger.

"I did not authorized this! If I did, wouldn't you think that I would be there to view the proceedings myself?!"

"Miss Ryder we don't spend all of our time being so cautious of legal documents signed by attorney and judges," replied Keith, "I thought that you couldn't make it because of some case you were working on. I've seen your signature often enough to know what it looks like, and it looked perfectly in order to me. I had to let Ricky go with this guy. I'm sorry. I had no idea it was a fake."

"I know it's not really your fault, James. Still, I would have preferred a phone call from you in order to confirm something like this. Now, I need to know who this scientist is and what business he had with Rick. I would also like to know who he works for and where his company is. I'm going there right now."

"All I know is that his name is Patrick Sandlak. He works for some genetic engineering firm. He wanted Meyers as a volunteer for testing something, I'm not sure. I don't know where could reach him or where he works."

"I need to contact this person right away and tell him bring him back here. Now, you're telling me that don't even have a number for his company? How can you expect Rick to be brought back now?"

"Like I was trying to tell you, he had an extraditions warrant with what looked like your signature on it. What else could I have done? If I didn't give him Rick, he probably would have dragged my ass in court, whether the document was legal or not."

"If anything bad happens to Rick, I will personally do exactly that. For all I know, this scientist could have a professional kidnapper trying to get ransom money from me. I can think of a million different things that could be happening to him right now. Trust me when I say, you will hear from me again. You better hope for your sake that I'll have good news to report."

Janiece's mind was racing. What about Jason? How was he going to react to this news? He was probably going to feel even worse now that his father was nowhere to be found. What was she going to say to him?

*　*　*

Jason was waiting for Janiece as she made her way slowly back to parking lot. She always asked him to wait inside her

39

car for her to return to let him out. She saw him looking up from the passenger window of her car, looking hopeful at the prospect of being able to come out and greet his father like they usually do, but this time was going to be different. He looked at her as he seemed to notice that something was different with Janiece as she came back with a handful of papers in her arms. She got inside the car, put the papers in the backseat, stuffed the key in the ignition... and stopped. She sighed, put her head on the wheel, and made sure not to look at Jason.

"Are you okay?"

She looked up and shook her head, and Jason could see that she was crying. Something was wrong.

"I'm sorry, sweetie. I'm afraid we're going to have to take a rain check. Your father is missing. I just don't know where he is any more."

"He's not in there?"

"Somebody took him for some sort of science experiment, or worse. I don't who or why, but they just took him and I don't know what's going to happen to him."

Jason seemed devastated by that news, and Janiece couldn't stop crying. She was ashamed of herself. She was supposed to protect Jason and his father, and now Rick was missing and his son couldn't see him anymore. How could she be a responsible mother to Jason? How could Jason trust her now, when she couldn't keep her promises to him?

Unfortunately, there was nothing she could do about this situation. The person who took Rick obviously knew what he was doing, and had the resources to pull off this subterfuge. She had to figure out what to do next. The only person who could help her now, was Joseph Henry.

Chapter 8

Daisy Carter found herself enjoying working as a medical researcher. BIOGENCORP felt like a tightly-knit community. She felt like she was back in college. It wasn't just work, it was something more. She felt like she was making something out of her life. Everything felt right with the world..

Like in a college dormitory, there were things left to freshmen. It was a bit of a tradition at BIOGENCORP to have the new employee stay overtime and run a defragmentation program on all the computers. It was as a way to get familiar with the computers, but it was also a way to put the new guy/girl through their paces...and in their place. Daisy didn't mind, tough, because the lab's computers ran with the most advanced software she had ever seen. They weren't running on Windows or Macintosh, but an independent software called NETREK. The software was designed by one BIOGENCORP's subsidiaries, after which the software was named. The speed with which the computers ran blew her mind away.

Daisy had to make rounds throughout the building after everyone else had left, checking every computer to make sure the hard drives was never interested in tedious work, but she was curious when one of her colleagues told that the defrag wouldn't last longer than two hours and a half. Never in her mind did she imagine that that would be possible. Still, she was glad that she had a book to read with her whenever she was sitting still.

The defrag was going so well, it almost didn't need Daisy's attention. She would look over her book every once in a while and check the percentage of completion on each of the monitors to make sure they were synchronized, and they always were. If they weren't, then the defrag process would slow down to a crawl, and she would have to intervene.

She was caught off guard when she heard an alarm coming from one the monitors. It wasn't something she was warned about, so she figured the other employees wanted to make sure she knew was she was doing.

Peeking at the screen, she saw that there was a message on the screen telling her that a file needed her permission in order to be deleted. The file's status read as CORRUPTED, which seemed odd, seeing as it was still there. Not only that, but usually, a defragmentation wasn't supposed to involve the deletion of files in their entirety. She was, of course, given an administrator's password, but she never expected to have to use it.

The file's name sounded familiar to Daisy. That name was often being mentioned in the staff lounge by her colleagues. It was supposed to be this huge project that certain, more experienced scientists were working on. She had always wanted to know what the project was all about, because it sounded like it was something really important.

She just couldn't help herself. She had to know what this was all about. She took one of her blank CDs and quickly made a copy of the file. Little did she realize what she had done could change the future of mankind.

Chapter 9

Wednesday, October 28ᵗʰ, 1998, 9:56 AM
Henry's Law Firm

Kirk Hall wasn't just another employee at Joe Henry's office. Not to him, anyway. He had slightly more experienced than most lawyers there, and therefore he got the most high-profile cases. Unfortunately, he always seem to win because of some technicality or another. It often got him into verbal altercations because he had a nasty habit of showing off.

"I don't want to hear excuses from you, Ryder."

"Stop calling me that. You know I hate it. And I won't let this go, either. Because you made that motion, Rick Meyers went to jail. Now, for some reason, somebody got a hold my signature and used it to have him extradited. Jason had already lost his father because of you, now nobody knows where he is. I could just tell this is killing him."

"It's not my fault you can't keep tabs on your clients. Anyway, who's to say that you didn't sign that paper yourself?"

"Because I would've been there to sign for it on the very day he was released!"

Sandlak had actually gotten in contact with Hall about getting Janiece's signature. Hall had taken a paper that she had signed the previous week and proceeded to forge her

43

signature. He never expected her to react this way. What could she possibly be complaining about?

"Your client's out of jail. You were the one who kept pestering me about his so-called innocence, so what more do you want?"

"How about the knowledge that he's alright? Now, I'm going to find out where he is, and when I do, I'm going to know who tried to use both me and my client like this. I'm going to go after him, and then, I'm going to teach you a little lesson in being a lawyer."

"Miss Ryder!"

Joe Henry appeared from the doorway of his office. His stern face made the bickerers stop dead.

"I would like to see you in my office, please."

*   *   *

Janiece's world was crumbling down around her. She was certain to be losing her job. She had already lost her client. She really didn't want to find herself in her boss's office again, especially not having to be there twice for the same reason.

"I know that you're feeling lost right now, but it's never a good idea to pick a fight with an empty suit. If you do, it will fill up with hot air enough to burn you. Let's just focus on what's really important, like finding Jason's father and figuring out what happened there in the first place. Incidentally, I understand how the little one might be feeling right now."

Henry smiled and Janiece knew he was talking about his own son, who disappeared about three years ago. Thankfully, Henry's son was eventually found, but Henry had gone through a six-week hellish roller-coaster of emotions, wondering what had happened to him.

"Jason is really trying to make me feel better instead of telling me whether or not he feels hurt. For some reason, he can't really see that he's the one who's missing his father, and that he should be devastated right now. I really want to find out what happened. I'm sorry, I guess I lashed out at Kirk for nothing. Lots of good that did."

"Forget about him. Kirk does his job with no emotion in mind. He searches for the win ruthlessly, which makes him a very good lawyer, but a lousy person to talk to or even be around. I've told him that, and I'm going to let you off with a little advice: You need to find evidence before you can accuse someone of foul play, and give your emotions the right kind of control."

*   *   *

Kirk Hall, meanwhile, was completing his paperwork, confident that he had just managed to put Janiece Ryder in the proverbial doghouse with the boss. Now, it was time for him to get back home, relax, and then go to his favorite restaurant, the *Royal Pallet*. The phone in Ryder's office started ringing. He would usually just leave it be, but he figured he'd play nice for as long as he was there, and answered.

"Henry's law firm, Janiece Ryder's office."

"Hello? I'm sorry. Are you Janiece's secretary?"

Her SECRETARY? Hall was never more insulted in his life. He had half a mind to tell this woman off and slam the receiver on her, but he refused to give Janiece Ryder an excuse to have him reprimanded, or even fired.

"No ma'am, I'm one of her colleagues. Miss Ryder is speaking with her boss at the moment. May I help you?"

"Yes, please. I'm going to fax something to her right now. Can you please tell her it's very important and give it to her right away?"

"Of course."

He hung up, then started waiting for the fax to arrive. Her secretary, she called him. So much for playing nice. Who did

Ryder think she was, anyway? She should be HIS secretary for all she was worth as a lawyer.

The fax took a good deal of time to print out, which meant that there were a lot of pages to go through. When it finally showed up, it gave Hall a shock. It was a twenty page monstrosity, and the name on the file was A.R.EX.. He realized there would be trouble for some of his clients. He had to act fast if he was going to warn them. He quickly photocopied the fax, then put the original on Janiece's desk with a note telling her about it. She could pick it up herself later on herself. He left an hour later, and contacted his clients about the new problem that arose.

Chapter 10

Rick Meyers was feeling a little uncomfortable about the situation he found himself in. His gut told him something was wrong, or about to go wrong. Why weren't Janiece and Jason there to see him off when he left prison? Why weren't they there to greet him when he arrived there? Did they even really know where he was? How could they not know? Janiece had to have been informed of his extradition. He just wasn't sure what he was doing there.

They had walked a long corridor on the third floor, leading to a huge chamber. Patrick Sandlak made conversation by commenting on how proud he was of the building, and the company. He explain that the company was going through a rebuild when he first arrived. He then described how long it took to build the two-story chamber, which was off-limits to anyone but staff members who belonged to a certain group. While building the chamber, they had gutted out a huge section of the third floor ceiling, but left a wide fenced ledge and door through which people could walk around, but otherwise left both floors in the chamber independent an inaccessible to each other.

Rick felt like the vast explanation was meant for someone other than him. He just wasn't sure if he really needed to take in all of that unnecessary information. What was the point of knowing all of this if he was only going to stay there for a short amount of time? Why didn't Sandlak tell him exactly what it was he was supposed to do? All he knew about his current situation, was that he needed to go through a check-up, just to make sure he was medically fit.

Sandlak was busy describing his life's work, and he didn't seem to notice that he was barely being listened to. He had so much lip momentum, Rick thought it was a miracle that his whole mouth wasn't running away, leaving his body behind. He was hoping the he could also be talking like that one day.

* * *

He was given a bedroom with a hotel-like feel to it. The furniture was simple, with a Victorian theme to it. It seemed a bit extravagant, considering he had to get used to prison mattresses and his &*$@#! cellmate.

Two days later, after performing custodial task apparently ordered by the state, he was given a full physical and medical evaluation. He was asked what food he liked and served his preferences, but the food tasted of sterility, ammonia, like the smell of the building itself.

He quickly gulped down his latest meal and took a cold shower in the adjacent bathroom. Afterwards, he settled down on the bed, feeling drowsy. Too drowsy.

He was falling asleep pretty fast for someone who just took a cold shower. His limbs were stiff and failing him, but why?

And then it hit him. The food! They must have drugged his food with some sort of sleeping agent. For some reason, they didn't want him conscious. Panicking, he tried to get off the bed, but only managed to fall to the floor before seeing his world fade away to nothingness

*   *   *

Patrick Sandlak was in his office, working overtime, which he had being doing often ever since Mark Reeves had left him in charge of the company so that he could take a vacation to the Bahamas with his family. The paperwork was always there, ready to remind of its presence. If he ignored it, then it would start piling up faster than normal. Thankfully for him, he didn't have a family and his social life was pretty much meaningless.

On his desk, Sandlak saw what looked to be a copy of his A.R.EX. file that was photocopied. Why would this be on his desk. On the stack of pages, was a note saying that Janiece Ryder, Meyers' lawyer, had a faxed copy of the file in her possession!

How could that have happened? There shouldn't have been any way for her to have that file. On top of that, she was Meyers' attorney. If she ever caught a whiff of his being here... no that was not an option. His project was his life's work, his ticket to a perfect world he'd been dreaming of for years. He had to find some way to change this situation and turn it in his favor. He dialed Kirk Hall's number.

"Hello? Thank you for the memo you sent me. Tell me, can you send me information on Janiece Ryder,? Much obliged, thank you."

He then started off towards the operating room to set his newly hatched plan in motion. Meyers was already unconscious, and was cleared for testing. It felt ironic to him that Janiece Ryder's fears where all going to come true soon enough.

Chapter 11

BIOGENCORP's third and fourth floor had a few renovations made to it in recent months. The entire eastern wing of the building on those floors had been hollowed out, and remade into an operating room. The room was filled with computers and monitors. There, it was told, was where the world would change.

And it had already changed. The A.R.EX. project had finally concluded its first successful test. Patrick Sandlak finally had a good reason to smile. His hard work had paid dividends, and now he could set his plan in motion.

The A.R.EX. project was his brainchild, so to speak. A.R.EX. stood for Anthropomorphic Reptilian Exo-Skeleton. The project's goal was to start by creating a squadron of 15 reptiles to be used as soldiers in military operations. These beings were to be put into service by the military, acting in covert operations where secrecy was the key to success. Not only that, but Sandlak theorized that they could also be used in an open battlefield should enough of them be eventually produced.

Erickson Meyers was chosen for the project because of his

skills in Aikido, which he learned at an early age and achieved the rank of third dan black belt. If that wasn't enough, but Sandlak really wanted to see whether or not his serum could actually have healing properties. What was changed, was that Meyers himself was no more. His body and mind where now new entities, transformed into an A.R.EX. soldier that was able to recognize his surroundings, but had no personal memory of who or what he was.

Sandlak was proud of the Mind Shifter, his patented key to the human brain. By using this specialized computer, he could peer into anyone's mind and change, add, or erase anything he saw fit. The brain used electric signals much the same way a computer's motherboard would function. Like a computer, the human brain would put together the different signals it received. Every signal had a place to go or come from. The Mind Shifter had done Sandlak a great deal of good.

Using the Mind Shifter to erase Meyers' personal memories by severing several neural connections in the temporal lobes, Sandlak felt he would then be able to mould the transformed creature as he desired. He was careful not to touch his general knowledge or other basic abilities such as motor skills, vision, and hearing.

The idea behind the process was to avoid the pain of announcing death to loved ones, and also create a soldier who would never hesitate before going out on the field. It would be much easier to send these beings that nobody knew or cared about into battle and not have to worry about them sacrificing their lives for whatever reason.

Erickson Meyers was no more. Instead, there was a formidable and intimidating creature. This being sported thick, leathery, black hide typical of a Gila monster, but he had a tall, lanky frame, which was much like Meyers'. His larynx, now repaired thanks to a regeneration gene commonly found in a Salamander, would hopefully be able to function. To make him look even more intimidating, instead of yellowy-orange blotches on his skin typical of Gila monsters, the new being had a bright-yellow lightning bolt pattern on his limbs, across his back, and encircling his head. A mane of jet-black hair had grown and now reached all the way down to his shoulders and his teeth were a lot sharper than a human's. His extremities had long, hard, pointed nails, almost like claws. Sandlak didn't bother cutting them. They would be good for shredding flesh apart.

Sandlak and his colleagues brought the being to the bedroom on a gurney, where Sandlak waited for it to wake up. He didn't have to wait very long, as the creature started to move its limbs. Its eyes flickered, and there was a slight moan. Suddenly, the being woke up and sat upright, rubbing its head and its eyes, as if waking up after a night's sleep. Sandlak saw with mild surprise, that his eyes were aquamarine colored.

Sandlak was a little nervous about how the being would react when it woke up for the first time. There was always the chance that it wasn't going to be too happy about finding itself in a strange room with a strange person sitting next to it. There was also the slight chance that the Mind Shifter didn't do its job, and that it was Erickson Meyers sitting there on the bed looking at him.

He knew that if he could get this being to trust him, then his plan would be successful right away. He would start by asking it a few simple questions, hoping his creation could speak and understand him.

"Hello," said Sandlak.

"Hello," replied the being, its voice deep, soft, and calm. There was no evidence that it was in any way suspicious of its situation or its surroundings. Sandlak eased his way into a conversation.

"Do you have any idea where you are?"

The being looked around, trying to get its bearings. Its

movements were slow and hesitant, its eyes slowly going from one side of the room to another, trying to find familiarity in its surroundings.

"I'm in some sort of room...perhaps a bedroom?"

"Correct. In fact, you are in our only bedroom. You are in a genetics facility. Do you know what that is?"

"No. Why am I here? It can't seem to remember..."

"Now, don't worry, I will explain everything to you, so ask away."

"What's my name?"

"Your name is Arex. You are a brand new being I've just created here in this lab. You will be put to service for the American military starting two days from now. For now, we must asses your physical, psychological, and medical states to make sure everything is fine, okay?"

"I suppose so."

Arex's voice was a little raspy and hesitant. Sandlak noted that there was a human quality to it, though not quite as recognizable, which meant that it was probably a remnant of Meyers' own voice as it was before his accident.

After helping Arex off his bed, the two set off to the medical wing Sandlak had set up for the project's "volunteers". After several physical and cognitive tests, Arex was cleared to be put to work. Sandlak figured had he had plenty of time to find Janiece Ryder and silence her for good.

Chapter 12

Thursday, October 29ᵗʰ, 1998, 2:24 PM
Janiece Ryder's Apartment

Janiece was going through a lot of stress even though she took a week's sabbatical from work as per her boss's request. A she left she saw that she had received a stack of faxed papers from her friend Daisy. She was wondering at first, whether or not it was some sort of practical joke, but as she read through the pages, she realized that it was much too elaborate for a prank. A phone call to Daisy confirmed it was no joke, and that it had her best friend was terrified.

The details of this project were horrifying. They sounded like something out of a horror movie, or a bad comic book. Janiece wondered how anyone could be a sick as to even try and pull something like that off, let alone find someone stupid enough to volunteer for such an experiment. This had to be illegal, and Janiece was worried because Daisy found herself tangled in all of that just because she got curious.

Janiece had to tell Joe Henry about it, but there one slight problem: even if BIOGENCORP had the technology and the knowledge to run a project this grotesque, they were being funded by the Pentagon, the very headquarters of the American military. The staff there represented the nation's entire defense system. Everyone working there had strong political and legal ties. The entire country, even the president would be implicated one way or another if this project was exposed to the masses. There would be a massive military and political upheaval not unlike what happened during the 1970s.

Not only that, but the legal implications were severe. If the project was exposed, then BIOGENCORP would probably deny that it even existed, claiming that the entire scandal was a hoax designed to scare the population. Even Janiece, who had read the file, couldn't really believe in it. Daisy would also get in trouble if word of this got out. She would be sue right out of her clothes for being so ready to share some of her employer's confidential information with one of her acquaintances.

In the new mess she found herself in she completely forgot about Rick Meyers. Jason's father had been missing for two days now. There had been no word of him back at the penitentiary, and Joe Henry's efforts to locate him were in vain. Law officials had decided to chalk it up as an escape ploy in which Rick was the ringleader. This couldn't have come at a worse time, as she had prepared his latest appeal. Janiece had promised Jason that she would find him, but she didn't even know where to look for him. He could be anywhere on the globe. What if something happened to him? She would never be able to explain this to Jason.

Her doorbell rang, taking her out of her reverie. Jason went and opened the door for her. He answered the door to a woman in a professional suit and suitcase.

"Hi, can I please talk to Janiece Ryder? Is she here?"

"That would be me. Please, come in."

Janiece made coffee for them while her visitor seated herself down.

"My name is Mika Nomura. I represent the FBI. I'm investigating BIOGENCORP."

"Really? Thank you. This is great news."

"It is? What do you mean?"

"It means you probably know about the A.R.EX. project. Daisy contacted you, didn't she?"

"I'm sorry, the what project? I've never heard of anyone named Daisy."

Janiece sighed. She was sure that Daisy had called the FBI asking for their help with the A.R.EX. file. But if the agent wasn't there because of that, what was she doing in her apartment? She gave the agent her cup of coffee and quickly went to her desk and took out her copy of the A.R.EX. file out of her filing cabinet. She figured if Mrs. Nomura wasn't here for that reason, she could at least hear her out.

"Here it is. This file contains everything I know about the A.R.EX. project. My friend, Daisy Carter came across this information. Before you read it, though, I would like to know why you're here."

"You see miss Ryder, we are here to ask you some questions about one of your clients."

Janiece hoped she wasn't talking about Rick.

"Which one?"

"Erickson Meyers."

"Have you found him? Is he alright? They kidnapped him, didn't they?"

"Actually, I was trying to work undercover on a case involving possible corruption in BIOGENCORP. I was called upon to visit the Penitentiary where Mr. Meyers was located. There, I was given the task to translate everything your client said by Chief Scientist Patrick Sandlak. He asked Mr. Meyers to volunteer for testing an experimental drug that could possibly repair any human tissue. He presented a court order signed by a judge and yourself, of course. Naturally, this looked really suspicious. I suspect Dr. Sandlak of having contacted you and offering you a deal on your client's behalf. I have to investigate all the leads here, so now I have to ask what your story is, since the judge who's name appears on the document insists on never having met you. I hope you recognize, as a lawyer, that you are in big trouble. You will be prosecuted to the fullest extent of the law, no matter how innocent Mr. Meyers seems."

First, Janiece loses her client to a kidnapper with a PhD, then she came that close to losing her job in a fit of rage, and now she was being accused of having cooperated with her client's kidnappers. Could things get any worse?

"Mrs. Nomura, I have no idea about some experimental drug, but I do know that I was never contacted by Mr. Sandlak, or any of his potential associates. My signature was forged. By whom, I don't know. If I were to participate in getting a temporary release for my client, I would've been there myself to survey the proceedings. This is exactly what I told James Keith, the warden. My client should still be in his cell right now, awaiting his next appeal, which was supposed to be today. I don't even understand Dr. Sandlak's motives for having taken my client out of all people. Is it possible that your case and this file I received are related?"

Janiece gave the file to the agent, who read through it. Her Asian eyes grew wide as she read.

"Who gave this to you," she asked, "is this some sort of joke?"

"I'm afraid not. Like I said, Daisy works at BIOGENCORP as a medical researcher. She managed to get her hands on this file, which she was supposed to erase while cleaning up their computers. I don't believe she's involved in this crazy scheme, but I haven't been able to do anything about this file before you knocked on my door. If word of this project gets out, the scandal that will ensue will tear the nation apart and put Watergate to shame. Now that I think about it, I'm starting to believe that Rick will be forced to be a guinea pig for Dr. Sandlak. If Sandlak is successful, than Jason will lose his father for good. I hope you can do something about this situation, because this might affect the world as we know it. I don't know who else to turn to. Please, believe me when I say I am not involved. Bare Hill's warden, Mr. Keith, will testify that I was there, not two hours after Rick was kidnapped, looking for him."

There was no telling what was going through the agent's mind. Did she believe her? Could she afford not to? What could she do with that kind of information? Just when she thought that she had an answer to her prayers, now she had to contend with another set of questions that had no answers. Why would Sandlak choose such an ordinary person like Rick? He didn't have any money, a physical description that narrowed down less than half a given population, and he couldn't speak a single word to boot. There were so many other prisoners, most of whom could probably be seasoned criminals, it just didn't make sense, especially since Rick's case wasn't even that well-known, despite its extensive media coverage.

"Can I have a copy of these pages, please?"

"Wouldn't you want the original fax?"

"No. You need to keep these with you. Right now, they may yet be the only clue to finding your client."

Janiece agreed, and gave the agent a copy of the fax she had received. Agent Nomura left, with a promise that they would keep in touch. Now all Janiece had to do, was wait and see what would happen next.

Chapter 13

Saturday, October 31ˢᵗ, 1998 1:04 PM
Abandoned Apartment, New York City

Arex suddenly found himself alone in an abandoned apartment building somewhere in a city called New York. It had been three days since he first woke up and he was deemed ready by Patrick Sandlak and his staff for his first mission as an American soldier. It seemed strange to him that he would be performing a military operation on his own, inside the borders of the country he was supposed to be serving. It was even stranger to him when he was simply given an envelope, a handgun, a map, a week's worth of rations, and was simply told to read the contents of the envelope.

Arex peered into one of the apartments. It smelled awful and dirty, as the entire building seemed to be rotting to its core. He sat down on a wooden chair, with his tail somewhat wrapped around his waist, a habit he quickly picked up. He set the envelope on a nearby table, opened it, and began reading. As he read on, he realized that he was being ordered to kill someone. His target was a woman named Janiece Ryder.

Sandlak had written up a profile on Janiece Ryder, depicting her as a lawyer working in a district of New York called Manhattan. She usually took the defense side of a case that she decided to work on.

Where the file got stranger was when it came time to find out the reason why he should kill her. Apparently, she was working for Mafioso, whomever they were, and often would represent them and have them acquitted for various reasons other than their innocence. She was also able to "silence" witnesses herself by ending their the he was now told to end hers.

Arex was most surprised when he saw her photograph. Her features were fair and she looked well-kept and serious, yet she was smiling. There was something about her that he found attractive.

He just couldn't understand why he had to kill her. He didn't know her. He didn't even know anybody, for that matter. Nothing in Janiece Ryder's photo gave him a whiff of any wrongdoing, no matter how small. Still, he figured that he had to do this, no matter what his feelings in the matter were. It's what he was created for, wasn't it?

That afternoon, Arex was laying down on a small mattress he had in another apartment. He was supposed to do away with Janiece Ryder as soon as possible, but he just couldn't bring himself to do it in his head. How then, could he do it for real? Whenever he thought about taking out his gun and pulling the trigger, he felt terrible inside. Was he just nervous? There had to be some reason why he was hesitating. What was his purpose for doing this? Why was he there? Does a soldier really have to be deployed to care of a supposedly rogue lawyer? Wouldn't there be a better suited authoritarian force for this situation?

Uneasy, Arex decided not to think about it too much and simply try to do as he was told, although it was going to prove to be very difficult. He was going to wait until nighttime, and try to sleep until then.

* * *

6:07 PM
Janiece Ryder's Apartment

Janiece Ryder was trying to settle down and watch the evening news. There was nothing on Rick's disappearance yet. She simply couldn't concentrate on anything else. She felt ultimately responsible for the safety of Jason's father and she had let them both down. Rick had always wanted to be assured that Jason would be taken care of in the best possible way. She wondered if they were too late in saving him from Sandlak and his insane project. She couldn't imagine what the Mind Shifter computer could do to someone once it was used. If and when that project would become public knowledge, there was no doubt that it was going to spark a public debate and a huge scandal, and all of it for what? A crazy military scheme. And what about the soldiers that would be created from this? They would be created to kill, so what would happen if they decided to go rogue? And what if they became injured or get too old to serve under law? Would they simply be done away with? Could people really be this cruel? Those many questions were making her head spin to breaking point. She knew that she wasn't going to be able to answer these questions right away, so all of these thoughts were simply going to distract her until the answers came to her one way or another.

* * *

9:15 PM
Abandoned Apartment

The job was so simple. All he had to do was kill someone who had murdered people in cold blood, without a single other thought. He imagined her taking out a gun and shooting people and then laughing about it, but it just didn't stick in his head long enough to be remembered. He probably tried to kill her so many times and failed. He would arrive at her door and knock casually. She would answer the door, take a quick look at him and scream in terror, realizing what he was. He pounces forward, his hand covering her mouth. Knocking her down he would then claw at her inside until he would slash her throat open. He would watch as the blood would start gushing out of her neck as her eyes looked on in horror as the life slipped from them...

Arex blinked for half a second and found himself alone in a black void. Janiece Ryder was gone. Her corpse left no blood, in fact it looked like there was nothing for Arex to stand on. A complete void, just like his mind.

"She's not here."

He turned around to face a woman wearing a pink bathrobe. Her red hair was curly and worn at shoulder-length. She looked really angry. She held something in her arms. It was a thin book. The title stuck out in bold letters: *The Amazing Spider-Man.*

"You gave me your word," she said.

"What?"

"You promised me you wouldn't do something like this."

"What are you talking about? Who are you?"

"You promised me you wouldn't do something like this! How could you? You made a promise and then you went back on it."

But he hadn't done anything. Not yet. Who was she? Why was she angry at him?

"I don't understand. What did I ever promise you? Do I even know you?"

"I'm so disappointed in you. You're a monster, and I will never forgive you."

She turned around and started walking away from him, her body becoming more and more transparent until it finally vanished into thin air.

"Wait! No! Come back! I was only told to do this. Please, come back!"

Arex's eyes flew open. He quickly sat up, sweat pouring down his face. He was still in the abandoned apartment, on the ragged mattress he tried to fall asleep on. Who was that woman? Was she even real, or was she a figment of his imagination? No, she couldn't be. The memory of her was too vivid. Memory? That couldn't be right. The memory of what? Who? What if he used to be someone else? What if Patrick Sandlak had lied to him? Would he really be that kind of person? Was he being used for someone else's profit? Why? How did Janiece Ryder fit into all of this?

All of a sudden, he started having so many questions. Never until now, did he have any reason to question Sandlak's motives or the task he was given to do. What could he do, now? Would he actually kill someone in the state he was in?

Was he really a monster? Why would he be a monster? If he killed Janiece Ryder, then maybe he...

Arex couldn't stand it any more, he had to get out of the apartment. He got out through the back door, leading to a metallic staircase that lead all the way to the roof. He climbed to the top of those stairs and looked around. He could see the huge green statue that was written on the map as "Statue of Liberty" and several tall buildings known as skyscrapers looming in the night sky. Miss Ryder was probably asleep by now. Should he go to her house? What would he do once he got there, wake her up...kill her? Janiece Ryder's apartment was located about five or six blocks away from where he was. Either he was going to kill Janiece Ryder or warn of the imminent danger that she was in. Either way, he was going to make his decision once he got there. He had to make that decision right away, because he couldn't spend an entire night with these thoughts and questions inside his mind. He only hoped that he would be able to make the right decision once he got there.

Chapter 14

Saturday, October 31ˢᵗ, 1998, 9:23 PM
New York City

Arex made his way across several rooftops, running across the rough pebbles on the flat roofs, leaping from one ledge to the next, and swiftly closing the gap between him and Janiece Ryder's apartment. All the while, he was still unsure of what he was going to do once he arrived at his destination.

He had originally intended to simply go out on the roof of the abandoned apartment building he was staying in and get some air, but this situation, was starting to drive him insane. The questions he asked himself and couldn't answer were making his head hurt and it wasn't helping him knowing that he was alone in an abandoned building with no one else to talk to.

He arrived at the ledge across the street from the apartment complex where Janiece Ryder lived. According to the information he was given, she lived on the fourth floor, in room number "404". Apparently he had to climb down into the alleyway in between the two buildings and enter through the parking lot in the basement. He made his way there, being careful not to be seen by anyone. Thankfully, it was fairly late in the evening and there no cars running to or from the parking lot. Arex figured that most people would probably be asleep. Arex entered the elevator and pushed the button for the fourth floor, then closing the doors using the switch rather than waiting for them to close. Once more, he surprised himself at being able to work an elevator, and actually recognize what an elevator was and what it was for.

He exited the elevator and found himself in a tight hallway. Number 404 was located at the end of the hall on the left side. As he got closer to the door, it felt like butterflies were invading his stomach. His hands started shaking when it got to try knocking on the door. His mind was a terrible mess he couldn't ignore. What was he doing there? How could he try to talk to a woman he never met, a woman he wasn't even sure would even be behind that door? What if he was walking into a trap. Who could he trust, Janiece Ryder or Patrick Sandlak? Wasn't it wrong to go against Sandlak's wishes and spare the woman her life, and warn her of the danger she was in? Wasn't it just as wrong to judge someone he never met and kill her without a second thought? He took a deep breath, moved out of the way of the peephole, and knocked on the door.

He had to wait for a good two minutes before he finally heard movement from inside the apartment. The doorknob turned slightly. Standing back against the wall next to the door, Arex felt his heart rate accelerate twenty-fold, and he tried to steady his breathing, fearing that Ryder would hear the beats from the other side of the wall.. The door opened towards the inside, and Janiece Ryder came out and started looking around...

Arex's instincts kicked in to high gear. Before he even knew what he was doing, he darted towards the woman with blinding speed, quickly putting his left hand over her mouth to keep her from screaming. He quickly dragged her inside the apartment, and closed the door with his foot as quietly as he could.

He held her in midair, holding her arms to her side with his right arm, to prevent her from punching him. He also wrapped his tail around her legs to keep them together. He waited for a while, listening for hints of anyone who might have heard their struggle. After a good while, he heaved a sigh of relief, somewhat confident that no one had heard them. Meanwhile, miss Ryder was struggling, trying to get away from him. Arex realized that, not only was she having trouble breathing, she was also bleeding from her arm, where he saw that he had accidentally scratched her. He had an idea when he noticed that the kitchen was just a short walk away.

He gently put her down so that she could support her own weight. He let go of her arms and put his finger to his lips to tell her to be quiet.

"Don't worry. I am not here to hurt you. If you promise not to yell for help, I will let you go. I just want to speak with you. Please, hear what I have to say."

She nodded in understanding and he let her go. He quickly stepped into the kitchen, ripped the short sleeve from his shirt, and wet it in the sink. He went back into the living room where he saw her sitting down on her couch, holding her arm. He quietly crouched down and started to apply the wet sleeve on her arm, being careful not to be too rough.

"I'm sorry," he said, "I didn't mean to hurt you. I just didn't want anyone other than you to see me just yet. I think it's best that we're alone right now."

"I could have sworn that you would have killed me the moment you saw me."

"It is what I was originally supposed to do. Somehow, I don't think it would have been a good idea. I just can't bring myself to even think about hurting someone, especially someone I don't even know."

He slipped the wet sleeve on her arm, tied a small knot with it, then sat down.

"Again, I'm sorry. I should have been more careful. I acted

under the impression that you would have been afraid of me, and I got carried away. I don't even remember half of what just happened in the hallway."

He was embarrassed to find himself here in the presence of someone he was attracted to from her photographs. He found her even more beautiful, but he didn't want to admit it.

* * *

Janiece sat there for a while looking at this being who basically just seemed to appear out of nowhere and was now sitting there, talking to her. If it wasn't sent here to kill her, what was it doing here? She had to find out what its intentions were soon. She couldn't have this thing stay here and eventually discovering Jason asleep in his bedroom.

"If you're not here to kill me, what are you doing here?"

"I'm not really sure of it myself. I'm a little confused. I read in a folder I was given that you were a corrupt lawyer and a murderer. Of course, I now believe that Patrick Sandlak was being less than honest with me. I don't how he could have expected me to kill you without a second thought. Do you know who Patrick Sandlak even is or what he does?"

"I do," Janiece replied, "and that's probably why you're here. You were created in as part of crazy scheme to have half-human half-reptile soldiers. I came across information on that project. Since the project was supposed to remain a secret, it's possible that Sandlak knew that I had that information somehow, and sent you here to stop me from making this information public. Unfortunately, I can't just release this kind of information to the public without any proof. I have to apologize about that, by the way, because if it weren't for the rules of the justice system I could've stopped this from happening to you, but I'm only one person with evidence that I shouldn't have in the first place, that was obtained illegally by one of my friends and given to me without proof. I'm only a lawyer, my head implodes just thinking about what might happen if I go public with this. Not only that, but nobody on this planet can possibly believe that something like you even exists without seeing you firsthand."

Janiece stopped and looked at the being who seemed to be thinking. It was an awkward moment before it spoke.

"It's possible that there will be more people like me, created from this project. If there would be a way to stop Sandlak, then maybe the project would grind to a halt. If only it were possible that you could stall the project and give yourself enough time to find your evidence the right way. There must be some sort of authoritarian group that's powerful enough to do just that. And if there's any way that I could help I would do anything you might want or need from me."

It was long shot, but Janiece thought that it might be a good idea. Who better to testify against Patrick Sandlak and bring him to justice than his own creation? What more proof could she possibly need? She knew that the first thing she had to do in the morning was talk to Mika Nomura, the FBI agent who came to her apartment two days earlier. She had given her a phone number to keep in touch.

"I think the authorities could use someone like you as probable cause to investigate BIOGENCORP, Patrick Sandlak, and the A.R.EX. project. That is, if you don't mind being a poster boy against this crazy scheme. And if you think you can stand speaking in front of dozens of people under the oath that you wouldn't lie."

"I think I'll be just fine. I don't think I will mind being used for something that doesn't seem dangerous. It seems a lot better than being lied to."

He stopped and looked behind Janiece. She wondered if there was something of interest, but it was just a shelf with a clock on it.

"It's very late. I think I better be going. Again, I'm sorry for having practically broken into your home."

"Where will you be going? Do you have any place to live, with a roof over your head? It's getting to be cold outside."

"There's an abandoned apartment not too far from here. It's where I was dropped off and told to find you. It's not really as cozy as it is here, but it'll have to do."

Janiece felt sorry for him. He had no memory, no life of his own any more. She decided that she had to help him like he promised to help her.

"Hold on, what's your name?"

"Arex."

"Like the project?"

"Yes."

"Well, Arex, if you promise not to snore too much, you can sleep here, if you want."

"Really? You wouldn't mind? Even after I hurt you?"

"I think you're really nice. I also think of what Sandlak might do to you if he finds out that not only you spared my life, but you also decided to help me in trying to stop him. You have to stay here, for your protection as well as mine."

She set up her couch as a makeshift bed and bid him good night. She figured that she had made the right decision, but she also knew that the moment everyone else knew about Arex's existence, and the existence of the project, there would be widespread panic all over the world. No matter what they did, the future was going to be in their hands.

Part 2

Confrontation

Chapter 1

Sunday, November 1ˢᵗ, 1998, 7:34 AM
Janiece Ryder's apartment

Arex had just spent a perfect, dreamless night, whatever was left of it. It was so incredible, he really didn't want to wake up. If he did, he feared that maybe he would actually be waking up in the old, beat-up apartment where Patrick Sandlak had dumped him a day earlier. He still couldn't bring himself to believe what happened during the night. He had actually worked up the courage to face Janiece Ryder and seemed to convince her that he meant her no harm...even though he managed to scrape her arm.

He didn't have the dream with the unknown woman, which was a good thing, but he was still confused about who she was and what she meant to him. Despite everything that was said between them, Janiece had let him sleep on her couch for the night. He was so thankful for that, he was now more determined than ever not to betray her trust or let her down.

He laid down, awake, but with his eyes still closed, hoping to open them only once heard her voice asking him to wake up. Suddenly, he heard a strange sound coming from nearby, maybe from within the apartment. It was barely audible, muffled from behind a closed door or behind a wall. As he sat up and opened his eyes he kept an ear out for that sound. It sounded like a piano of some sort playing softly. He stretched his arms and legs, got off the couch, and walked toward the sound.

The apartment had a small corridor where the bedrooms were. There were three doors, one of which Janiece entered when she went to bed. Another door was barely opened and showed him the bathroom. The third one was closed. Arex noticed that the sound was heard louder behind that door. Arex thought Janiece lived alone, but opening that door put an end to that idea.

There was a young boy sitting on a bed. In his hands, he was handling some sort of grey machine. Arex could only guess that the device was the reason for that piano-like sound.

The boy looked up...and saw Arex standing at the door frame. His mouth dropped and at the same time, he let go of the grey device. Arex held his hands up, hoping not to frighten the child.

"I'm sorry to bother you, I hope I didn't scare you," said Arex, "I just woke up and I heard a strange sound. I was wondering where that noise was coming from."

"I'm sorry, mister. I guess I was playing too loud."

Mister? Arex felt strange to be called mister. Then again, he had no idea how old he was. It was very possible he was older than the child, but he didn't feel all that old.

"Please, just call me Arex."

"Arex? That's a really cool name. My name's Jason."

Arex nodded. He looked around the bedroom, his eyes registering everything. The room was painted a dark blue. Jason's bed was up against the wall to the right. Opposite the bed was another machine with what he recognized as a screen and a keyboard. Who did he know these things? And then there was the filled bookcase in the corner next to a television set. He noticed that a lot of wires were laid on the floor.

Arex slowly edged himself inside the room, feeling comfortable that he wasn't scaring the boy anymore. Jason, meanwhile, picked up his dropped device and started touching it with his hand.

"Is it broken?"

Jason laughed at the question.

"This thing? I dropped it so many times when I was younger...right on the wooden floor. But it's a Game Boy. These things were built like bricks. Did you know one of these things survived an explosion during some war in the Middle East. It still works today. That was so incredible that they have it playing in a museum somewhere."

"Really?"

"Yeah. Wait, you never heard of this? Everybody who has one of these knows that."

"I'm sorry to say that I don't know much about anything. You'll have to forgive me, but I'm new to the world, if you know what I mean."

"You're an alien? Do you come from outer space?"

"I don't know anymore. It's more likely I was once human. The first thing I remember was waking up in a bedroom inside some company's building. I was told I was supposed to be a soldier."

"Awesome. You're like Wolverine or something. Did you escape from your creators? Do you have any idea who you were?"

"No. I plan on helping your mother bring them to justice."

"That's really cool. You're like, above everything like violence and killing people. Are you sure you're not a comic character who came out of your book?"

"No, that much is certain."

"That's cool. Well, if you want, there are comic books

that you can read. Most of them were my dad's. I'm sure he wouldn't mind if I let you borrow any."

Arex turned his eyes to the bookshelf in the corner of the bedroom. It was filled with comics books, each and everyone of them encased in what Arex guessed was a plastic sleeve. Somehow, he knew just what a plastic sleeve was and what it was used for. Arex looked at the titles on the covers of those who were thick enough to even carry a title there. As he looked at them, he sensed there was a pattern to the way Jason had placed them. They were alphabetized by the name of the main character, which usually found itself on the cover. Looking even closer, Arex could tell they were further classified chronologically from the earlier releases to the left, to the newer copies on the right.

"Some of these were made in the late fifties," Jason commented, "those ones are the rarest, and I never let anyone borrow them. They're gonna be worth a lot some day, and maybe, if I'm a dad, I'll have twice that many issues to pass down."

"That sounds like a dream. I hope it comes true for you."

"You wanna see my dad's all-time favorite?"

"I would. Thank You."

Jason stood up and searched the second to last shelf. He carefully read the labeled covers until he found the one he was looking for. Using both hands, he slowly slid the book from the shelf and showed it to Arex. Arex sucked in a gasp. The cover read: *The Amazing Spider-Man.* The cover was the exact same one he'd seen in his dream.

"I know this one. Or at least, I think I do."

"Yeah, it's the one where the Lizard appears for the first time."

"You don't understand. I don't know how, but this book cover is familiar to me."

"Well, if you want, you can borrow it and read it. Maybe you'll remember what the story is about."

As he was about to ask Jason another question, Janiece appeared in the doorway. Surprising to Arex, she was smiling.

"You two seem to be getting along well," she said.

"I didn't know you had a child," Arex replied.

"I wasn't sure how you would react to that. I adopted Jason a few months ago."

* * *

The truth was that Janiece wanted to protect Jason from Arex, because she still wasn't certain she could trust Arex. Could he be deceiving her? She couldn't tell by just looking at him. Arex's face was completely neutral and never gave any emotion away. Janiece had to rely on his voice, and that fact didn't make her feel too comfortable about her situation. Patrick Sandlak wanted her dead, and that meant that if Arex didn't kill her, Sandlak could probably create another soldier and send him after her. If that happened, Arex could be the only one able to protect her. It seemed that in a matter of days, she had managed to lose Jason's father, get herself involved in a matter of corporate corruption, and endanger not only her life, but the life of the eight-year-old kid she was supposed to nurture, teach, and protect. Could this get any worse?

She contemplated her worries until she witnessed the most bizarre of scenes. Jason, who seemed to be getting more and more comfortable around Arex, had just asked him if he wanted to try playing the Game Boy.

"The game is called Pokémon Red Version. Right now, this is the hottest game around. It came out about a month ago."

"I'm sorry? What does that mean?"

"It means that millions of people around the world are playing this game and its sister game. As we say it "Gotta Catch'Em All!"."

Arex took a look at the small screen on the Gameboy. The

image he saw was fuzzy and green. Even though the screen was small and blurry, he could clearly make out the image of a small man in the middle of the screen.

"You move the guy around with the cross on the left," said Jason, "you have to maneuver through the grass up to the building."

Arex concentrated his sight on the screen . He pushed the head of the cross down. The character responded by moving upwards. He had gotten about half an inch before the screen suddenly turned to black, and the music changed.

"What just happened?"

"You just entered a battle," said Jason reassuringly.

*   *   *

Jason went on, patiently guiding Arex through the game, step by step. Janiece thought it was strange that an adult would actually have the patience to learn a video game from an eight-year-old boy. There, she saw an aspect of parenting she knew she needed to work on. She smiled to herself. There was clearly more to Arex than met her eye.

Janiece cleared her throat loud enough for Jason and Arex to snap out of their game-induced reverie.

"If you two are finished being Pokémon trainers, I need to talk to Arex for a moment."

She had Arex follow her in her kitchen were Janiece had made breakfast for the three of them.

"I need to talk to you about something," she said.

"Is there anything wrong?"

"It's just that there's so much I don't know about you. There is a huge mystery surrounding you. I find myself second-guessing my decision to let you stay here. It's nothing personal, but I can't read you as well as I'd like."

""Read" me?"

"People tend to judge other people by what they see and

hear, but the sight usually has the advantage. Sometimes, you can tell a person's state of mind by looking at the expressions on their faces. Your face is neutral. I can't tell what you're thinking, so I can't make my mind up about you. And now, Jason's met you, and he already likes you."

"Is that a bad thing?"

"Jason's at an age where reality and fiction are still being defined. You've just blurred the line between the two by just being here."

"But I'm real, I can assure you."

"You are, it's just...I don't know."

She really didn't know how she felt. There was confusion, disbelief, anger, relief, happiness, and sadness all mixing her up inside. Janiece felt vulnerable, and she didn't want to show it. There was so much at stake. She couldn't expect Arex to understand her feelings. But then again, she had to remind herself that she couldn't understand Arex's feelings either.

It was probably frustrating for one to not be able to remember anything about one's past. Who was he? Did he have family, friends who liked him? What was his crime? Nothing about him was supposed to be personal. Instead of memories, there was a void that might never be filled. He was designed as a weapon, a living killing machine. What some people didn't realize, was that this weapon had a heart and feelings.

"Janiece, maybe it would be better if I left," said Arex, "I agree when you say that we don't know much about me. We can't ignore the fact that I might be a threat to the both of you. I can't imagine anyone else's reaction to my presence would be better than yours. I will leave tonight, and keep a low profile until you need me ."

That made Janiece very nervous. At least if Arex stayed here, she could keep an eye on him. She knew he was right in saying that there was no way to predict anyone's reaction to his existence.

Suddenly, an idea dawned on her. She had to have Joe Henry meet Arex. Her boss should be able to be a good gauge for future reference.

She had Jason dress up. They left Arex in the apartment. Janiece then dropped Jason at Kip Simon's place. She was comfortable in leaving Arex alone with nothing to do, but watch TV.

Chapter 2

Arex suddenly found himself alone in Janiece's living room and couldn't understand why. He had practically promised her that he would leave as soon as the morning settled, but she insisted on him staying here. And yet, Janiece wasn't very comfortable having him around. He couldn't imagine how she could possibly feel safer with the prospect of leaving him alone in her apartment and him being here when she came back.

He had been someone else once. When Janiece told him that, an entire other set of questions entered his mind. Shouldn't he remember being someone else? Who was he? What was he like? What was his name? He had to find some answers, and he just couldn't trust the person who sent him there to kill someone.

Janiece was having second thoughts about trusting him, of that he was sure of. He hoped he was wrong, though. If he was right, then he would have to find a way to let her see that there was nothing to be afraid of as far as he was concerned.

Janiece had given him the file on the A.R.EX. project the

night before, so that he could read it at his leisure. From what he read, he was able to piece together what he had become a part of. He was created from another person, whose memories were erased and whose genome was basically reconstructed. Who that person was, was unknown since it wasn't written in the file. His appearance and genetic structure were altered to the point that he would be unrecognizable when compared to his former self. His memories were wiped out thanks to a special computer known as the Mind Shifter. He was to be only one of many anthropomorphic reptiles that were to be created from this project. The idea was to create a squadron of beings like Arex that would be trained in covert operations, espionage, assassinations, and open warfare. Arex was disappointed knowing that there might have been more information on the project that didn't show up in the file, such as the composition of the A.R.EX. serum. It wasn't as if he was certain to be able to understand a chemical concoction, but he was curious as to what was now coursing through his veins as a result of a science experiment. He did feel a little angry at the thought of having been used as test subject for something that was potentially dangerous, and left without the memories of being a guinea pig among maybe others. That sparked another series of questions. What if he wasn't the first one? What if there were others like him out there? If there were others, what was Sandlak making them do?

He turned his focus back to the television set. His idea of having fun did not include staring at a glowing box with sound, but what else there to do? Nonchalantly, he pressed the button on the remote control to turn it on. When the screen came on, he was looking at something that defied belief. He saw what looked like a war going on inside a building. People holding guns and dressed in shiny white uniforms were chasing a man and a strange being that was very tall and hairy. The pair was chased through a door that closed automatically, leaving the soldiers in white frantically scrambling to open it. The scene cut to an old man being called to a fight with a masked being dressed all in black. A strange humming sound was heard from what looked like swords bathed in light. As the two people's blades clashed, Arex was awed. Who were these people? Why were they fighting? Was this some of event that happened?

Suddenly, Arex saw a story unfolding as the earlier pair were joined by two other people. The group watched intently as the men in white disappeared from their view. Two metallic beings, who were also watching the scene unfold, joined the group as they ran toward some sort of ramp. One of the people a young man, stopped and looked at the old man, fear gripping his face. The old man smiled and then appeared to vanish as he left himself be struck down by the dark being's sword.

The screen seemed to get bigger Arex's eyes were almost glued to it. He was jarred from the screen when the door suddenly opened. It was much too early for Janiece to be back. Someone else had the key to the apartment, but who?

Arex heaved a sigh of relief when he realized it was Jason. And yet he wasn't supposed to have been back until Janiece came back with him. The question was: was there a reason why he was here?

Arex turned his head. Jason was there, but he wasn't alone. Another boy was with him. The other child seemed to be around Jason's age. Janiece hadn't told him about the other boy, nor did he think she wanted anyone else to know about him yet.

The boy took one good look at Arex, and his mouth dropped. He then looked at Jason with a look of admiration and said:

"Dude, you are so lucky."

"I know, awesome, right? Arex, this is my friend, Kip."

"Hello," said Arex timidly.

"Hi," Kip replied.

Jason pointed at the TV screen.

"Cool, you're watching *Star Wars*."

"*Star Wars?*"

"Yeah, it's a great movie."

"A movie?"

"Yeah, a movie. It's not real, or anything."

"It isn't?"

"No. It's just actors and special effects. Really good actors and special effects, but that's it. This story never happened. That galaxy doesn't exist and neither do the people."

"Oh. I thought it was real. It's very believable."

He was distracted once more by the space battle that was raging on the screen. A few seconds later, though, it hit him.

"What am I doing? Jason, why is your friend here? Does Janiece know you're both here?"

"... No."

Jason and his friend bowed their heads, ashamed.

"I wasn't supposed to tell him? Are you gonna tell her? Are we in trouble?"

Arex sighed. He knew that the right thing, the safer thing to do, was to tell Janiece. He didn't feel it was right, however, to tell Janiece that her son had done something against her will. He also didn't want to leave Jason with the daunting task of trying to explain his bringing his friend to her apartment to show Arex off to him while she was away.

"We will tell her together. It is the right thing to do."

"Okay."

Arex then looked at Kip.

"You have to keep this to yourself. You can't tell anyone about me, do you understand?"

Kip nodded.

"Alright. I promise"

He had Jason and his friend leave the apartment. *Just in time*, he thought, as the phone rang in the kitchen. Thankfully, Janiece was just checking up on him, and was a long way from coming back. That was good, because he had no idea what to tell her once she returned.

* * *

10:45 AM
Henry's Law Firm

Janiece got to the firm's offices, and immediately accosted each of her co-workers to find out where Joe Henry was. Along the way, she ran into Kirk Hall.

"Whoa, Ryder, you're not supposed to be here. Shouldn't you be on sabbatical?"

"I need to talk to Henry now. It's urgent."

"Well, he's in a meeting, which is just as urgent. You're going to have to wait."

That was fine with her. She was willing to wait the few minutes, even though anxiety took hold of her again. She used the time to calm herself down before her boss arrived. Joe Henry was there within 15 minutes. He looked just as surprised to see her there. Janiece saw him give her a reproachful look.

"You're not supposed to be here."

"I know, but I really need to talk to you right away."

"What is it?"

How was she going to break the news to him? What could she say? She didn't want him to panic, but she also wanted him to know the full extent of what had happened last night. She wanted to start the conversation gently, but what she ended up saying was:

"There's a giant talking reptile in my apartment right now. It was created out of the A.R.EX. project."

"What?"

"I know it's going to sound crazy, but...here, look at this."

She took a photo of Arex while he slept that night. She took the snapshot out of her purse and handed it over to her boss. His eyes went wide as he looked at Arex on her couch.

"Is this thing real?"

"Yes."

"And it was sleeping in your apartment?"

"I let him sleep there. We met and we talked and…"

"Have you lost your mind?"

"Hold on, you don't understand."

"No, I don't. How can you let something like that anywhere near you? What about Jason?"

"Let me start from the beginning: he was sent here to kill me. Instead of doing that, he decided to warn me. He basically saved my life. What was I supposed to do but trust him and let him stay? The only place had to go to was an abandoned apartment."

"But now he knows where you live. And what about Jason's safety? You didn't leave the two of them alone together did you?"

"Jason's at his friend's house right now. I still know how to take precautions, that's one of the reasons why I'm here. I want to know what to do next."

"But why would somebody want to kill you?"

Janiece proceeded to explain the events of the last couple of days. Joe Henry took notes all the while. When she finished, he nodded in understanding.

"I need to see this Arex. If he's anything like you say, then maybe you have yourself a prosecution case with a real star witness. Incredibly enough, I'm very curious about this. You're saying that he has honest to goodness amnesia?"

"His memories were erased by a special computer. He was told by Patrick Sandlak that he was created in the project. Sandlak didn't tell him anything about his former self, probably for a good reason."

"Well, this comes against my better judgment, but let's go see the talking reptile."

Chapter 3

Mike Scatchard and Mika Nomura got to Janiece Ryder's apartment door. They needed more information on the A.R.EX. Project, and they hoped she could provide them with such. In truth, they were also a little suspicious of her claim that she knew nothing of Rick Meyers' extradition until it was too late. The likelihood of that happening was nearly impossible. The warden of Bare Hill corroborated her story, but added that she was extremely agitated and overemotional over one of her clients. It was possible she threw a fit at the prison to have suspicion placed as far away from her as possible. Even if she wasn't involved they had to have more proof than a stolen computer file in order to get a warrant to search BIOGENCORP's building.

Mike knocked on the door. They waited for a couple of minutes. There was no answer. They tried again, with the same result.

"I guess we have to pick the lock."

Mike took out his tools, and got to work on the lock. It only took him a few seconds before the door clicked open.

They entered the apartment. The TV was on in the living

room, displaying a talk show. A male voice called out from the kitchen.:

"Janiece? Is that you? Why were you knocking?"

"F.B.I. We have a search warrant for this apartment."

"F.B.I.? What does that mean?"

The owner of that voice came closer, the agents watched as he slowly stepped out of the cover of the wall.

Mika let out a gasp. There, standing in front of them, was a giant reptile, which she recognized as an A.R.EX. Soldier from the file.

"What can I do for you?"

It was talking to them. The agents exchanged some nervous glances. Mika pursed her lips and stepped forward.

"We came here hoping to find miss Janiece Ryder. You are obviously not who or what we were expecting."

"I can imagine. If you don't mind coming later, Janiece is at work right now. She did say she'd be back within the hour."

"Good, then we'll wait for her," Mike replied.

Now what? Now they were both confronted with a terrible truth: they were too late to stop an Arex soldier from being created. Not only that, but it was now in Janiece's living room. Why it was there, Mika had to figure out. Until then, the being was asking them questions.

"You two never told me what F.B.I. means. What exactly gives either of you the authority to break into Janiece's apartment like this? I hope you have proof of your being in a law enforcement organization. If you don't I won't mind throwing the both of out."

"We are federal agents," said Mika, "This is Mike Scatchard, my partner on this case, and my name is Mika Nomura. We are currently investigating BIOGENCORP in relation to the A.R.EX. project. We wanted to know whether or not miss Ryder could tell us something new."

"Perhaps you would like to take a look at the file? She told me herself, all the information she has is in there."

"No. Unfortunately, we already have a copy of that file from when I visited her not too long ago. She told me that she has a source who works at BIOGENCORP. That person provided her with the file. We were hoping something else would have come up that could give us more evidence."

"Isn't this file enough? At what about me? I'm proof enough of what happens to people who are transformed through the project."

"Yes, that's true, you would be a good addition to our evidence pile. A pile that's not very big, however, since we have reason to believe that the American military is involved in this scheme. If so, then that makes the project perfectly legal."

"Not if Patrick Sandlak created me will the sole purpose of killing Janiece."

That would have certainly tainted the legality of the project, but only if it could be proven.

"So that was Patrick Sandlak's reason behind changing the schedule of the project?"

"Apparently so. I know now that he was being dishonest with me."

"Why?"

"Janiece guessed it was because of the file she received. Sandlak told me, or rather wrote down that Janiece was a corrupt lawyer, who wasn't above murder to protect her clients. Something in that folder I read didn't sit right with me, so I decided I wouldn't do anything until she told me her side of the story. I believe she's the one who told me the truth. Not only that, but I suspect that even if she was a criminal, it shouldn't be my problem to solve, but rather someone in your position, am I correct?"

"That's right"

"And on top of that, ending people's lives shouldn't be

something I was meant to do. It doesn't feel like it would be a natural thing to do. Am I making sense, or am I just ignorant?"

"No, well, perhaps a little," said Mika. "Maybe you might be a little naïve, but it was a good idea to come clean about what you were sent here to do. Tell me, what's your name?"

"Patrick Sandlak named me Arex, after the project."

* * *

The agents looked at each other. Arex waited as they started making hand gestures and speaking inaudibly. It seemed to him that they were having a private conversation. Finally, the male agent took the lead.

"I hope you understand that your existence is going to cause a lot noise."

"Why? If there were many of me, I would understand, but there is just me."

"First off, you really don't know that at this point. Second, Your presence alone is actually enough to cause widespread panic on the face of the Earth."

"How can that be? Why is my existence such an event?"

"Think about it this way: Appearance plays a major role in perception and impression. We look at someone and we tend to base our impressions of that person on the way they look, it doesn't matter what that person is really like. Human beings also have a natural fear of the strange and the unknown. Someone like you can simply walk down the street and still cause widespread panic, you don't even need to say or so anything. Not only that, but let's take your specific case into light. The circumstances and motivations behind your creation are less than ideal. You were created to be a killer, a weapon, and now you suddenly decide to do otherwise? If, or rather when you'd be discovered there will be people who will question your motives and will perceive you as a threat. People might celebrate you, fear you, try to destroy you or maybe even worship you as some sort deity come from another world. On top of that, people like to put things and living beings into different categories. They would spend hours on end trying to figure out, not only who you are, but what you are. And I'm not even talking about a species in this case. There will be debates on whether or not you're a martyr, a criminal, a weapon, an animal, a person, etc. Some people might even try to create more of you or even become just like you. The entire face of the Earth could change over this matter, because..."

"ENOUGH!!!"

Arex found himself panting and sweating after the agent's speech. His hand trembling, he dragged himself to the kitchen to get a glass of water. He bent down on the sink, trying to calm his nerves down. How could he live knowing what his life was going to be like once people knew about his existence? Why did life have to be so complicated?

"Are you okay?"

The female agent had followed him in. From the look on her face, Arex guessed she was concerned about something. Was she concerned about him? Why?

"I'm not sure. I just couldn't even fathom all of these things. How can I continue? I wish I was never created."

"That's never a good reaction to have. I'm sorry, but it was necessary to tell you what might happen. Janiece was probably sheltering you from this truth because she might've guessed your reaction ahead of time. I can see how this is affecting you. You're crying."

Arex realized it was a fact as he felt under his eyes.

"It doesn't matter, anyway. I'm a monster, right? I don't have any feelings. What in the world gives me the right to have a say in what I do or what happens to me? I'm just a weapon meant to kill and not care."

"A weapon, maybe, but you're also a person who has a

genuine mind and a heart. Any intelligent life should be entitled to the same rights, privileges, and responsibilities as we have. You've taken responsibility by owning up to what you were supposed to do and deciding against it."

"Do you really believe that?"

"Yes. Don't pay all that much attention to what anybody says about you. You and you alone are the only person who can judge you adequately."

"But what if it's true, and all of these do happen? It would be my fault."

"You can't think like that. Sure there might a bit of a problem for you earlier on, but who's to say you can't live a normal life? People will slowly get used to you until they accept you and those you refused to do so will be thought of as backwards thinking."

The door clicked open right at that moment. Arex's mouth flew open as he looked at the agents.

"Oh no. It's Janiece. She's here."

They hurried back to the living room, where they found Janiece and another man coming in through the door. Janiece's mouth was just as wide when she saw the agents in her apartment. Arex felt embarrassed to be found in their company.

"Uhmm...I can explain," he said, but he realized that there was no way he could explain what had happened while she was gone.

Chapter 4

Sunday, November 1ˢᵗ, 1998, 11:45 AM
BIOGENCORP Laboratories

Patrick Sandlak was hard at work, trying to get a new, larger budget approved. There was no doubt that the A.R.EX. project was a viable cause, but the financial restrictions due to the other tasks BIOGENCORP was accomplishing, added to the limited budget the Pentagon was sending him, were getting in the way of being able to extradite the other prisoners he needed to complete his squadron, housing them and then having them transformed and then trained. The disastrous first test in July had done a lot of damage to his reputation and made his employers panic slightly about his ability to get the job done. He wanted to be able to complete the first squadron by the end of the year, the trouble was getting the money he needed.

At the same time, he was waiting for a report on Arex's whereabouts. He had sent an espionage expert to keep tabs on him. He had been told earlier that Arex wasn't at the apartment where he was dropped off. This might have meant that he spent the night at Janiece Ryder's apartment after silencing her.

In the meantime, Sandlak had to look into his technical

systems to make sure that they weren't tampered with. He also had to make sure that nobody made changes to his A.R.EX. file. He was the only person to know the specific details of the project, such as the inner workings of the Mind Shifter and the composition the serum used for the transformation. This meant that the project revolved around him. Not even his superiors knew that he had put a special alarm notification for the file in case it was intrusively accessed, deleted, copied, or even slightly modified. The specifics of the intrusion would be kept in his computer's log and pop up the minute his password was inputted into the system. Sandlak always checked the files once a week. It was his life's work, and he had to protect it.

His safe thinking was justified when he found a recent intrusion in the A.R.EX. file. It came from one of the main computers in the operating chamber. The log showed that the file was accessed and copied on the 27th. He realized that this is where Janiece Ryder got her source from.

He checked the duty roster for the 27th. It revealed that Daisy Carter was running the defragmentation program on all computers. What her relation to Janiece Ryder was, Sandlak didn't know. One thing was certain, she had to be silenced. When Arex came back, he would have him get her too.

The next phone call he received put paid to those thoughts. His spy described the comings and goings in Janiece Ryder's apartment. At one point, Arex was actually left alone for more than two hours. Not only that, but he had spent the night there. On top of that, there were now two FBI agents now in her apartment.

His project was no longer a secret, that much was clear. He was betrayed, and now his life's work was in danger of being destroyed. He had no other choice, but to step in and fix this problem himself.

Chapter 5

Sunday, November 1st, 1998, 12:00 PM
Janiece Ryder's apartment

Janiece just found herself in a real mess. All she wanted to do was show Arex to her boss, and now she had to contend with two F.B.I. agents. To make matters worse, Arex had let people inside her apartment without her knowledge or consent.

She tried to get angry at him, but it was hard because in the back of her mind, the thought of the fact that Arex was completely amnesic and somewhat naïve, so she figured he had to let them in. She was also somewhat innately afraid of him. That last thing was something she had to work on. She now hoped the agent's presence wasn't going to mean serious trouble or more bad news for her.

"I'm not mad Arex," she assured him, "I just wish I'd given you my cell phone number. And maybe I should have told you not to allow anyone inside. It's a good thing I recognize these agents, but you need to be careful from now on."

"They broke into your apartment. I'm sorry. What's a cell phone?"

"Later."

Just then, Jason came back from Kip Simon's apartment. Janiece heaved a sigh of relief.

"Jason, please go to your room. I have people here and we have things to discuss," she said.

"Wait," said Arex, "There's something else you should know. Jason came here earlier with his friend, Kip Simon."

Oh no, she thought, *he didn't just say that.* He just released the bomb and now she was going to exploded.

"WHAT?! How could you let them in the apartment?!"

"I didn't let them in, Jason had his key with him."

Of course he did, she thought. Now matter how she looked at it, Kip Simon was now involved.

"You don't really understand how bad this is, do you?"

"I'm not sure," Arex replied, "but I don't see how it can be that bad. Kip won't tell anyone. He promised me that much."

"You can't count on a eight year-old kid to keep a promise!"

"Why not?"

"Because most kids aren't mature enough to keep their mouths shut! Especially with something as important as the existence of a humanoid reptile here on Earth."

"Please, calm down," urged Joe Henry.

"I will not calm down! For all we know, you could've already fed what you know about Jason and Kip to Patrick Sandlak. I don't want to be killed, or worse!"

With tears in her eyes, Janiece looked at Arex. He had hung his head down, and she realized she had just told everyone in that room that she didn't trust Arex at all despite having just let him spend the night in her apartment and had just left him alone for two hours.

"Is that what you think? That I would betray your trust and put all of your lives in danger?"

"Maybe. I just don't think I trust you enough with anything. Please understand, you were created to be a weapon. With that in mind, I have to keep an objective perspective and not take our safety around you for granted. On top of that, your attitude is not normal. Nobody should be that calm about a situation like this. Normal people are never this honest, or this innocent."

"Do you think I'm being less than sincere? If you had doubts about me, why didn't you say so in the first place? I told you that I would leave last night after having talked to you. Why didn't you let me leave?"

"I don't know. It just that I want to be able to trust you. I just can't rely on my eyes to tell me whether or not your lying to me."

"I'm sorry. If you want me to leave right now, just tell me, and I will."

The truth was, Janiece wasn't sure distancing herself from Arex was the right thing to do.

"Do you know who gave me the information for the A.R.EX. project?"

"I have no idea."

"It was a friend of mine. Her name is Daisy Carter. She works at BIOGENCORP. She wasn't supposed to know about it, but she discovered the file on their computers and downloaded it."

"Why are you telling me this?"

"Because I'm going to learn how to trust you. I don't want to distance myself from you, because I know that people being afraid of you will cause you to feel ashamed or even angry at yourself. I just can't have my doubts interfere with my work Your thinking is different from ours because of your amnesia, I know that, and that's why your so innocent."

"I don't understand. Are you talking to me? Why would you say these things?"

"Excuse me, I was talking to myself, maybe trying to figure you out. This city, in this era, despite holding ties to others, is isolated in certain ways. You can tell the difference between someone from New York City and someone from, let's say, in the farmlands of Arkansas. It's just one of the reasons why humanity is so divided. You can guess where a person comes from the physical appearance, the language, the spoken accent of that language, the ethnical origins, and the religious or spiritual beliefs. You don't have any of those traits, which makes it even harder to figure you out. Nobody on this Earth in this day and age can relate to you in any. Knowing this, it's going to be really difficult for you go about announcing your existence to the world. And what would happen to you from there is entirely up to fate to decide."

"Well, everything about life seems complicated now, but I know that I can't remain a secret forever. Eventually, people are going to know about me, it's only a matter of time. I think it would better to stop Sandlak's project if knew about me sooner rather later."

The female agent, Mika Nomura, intervened.:

"Until then, we have to come together and work out something that will stop Sandlak and hopefully the project. Miss Ryder and Jason will have to come with us to a secret safe house. There, they will be better protected and no one outside of the F.B.I. will know where they are. Unfortunately, with a perfectly legal contract in their hands, there will be no stopping BIOGENCORP from creating even more reptilian soldiers and doing what they want with them. We need more proof."

A funny sound was heard nearby. It sounded like someone was chocking on something. Every head turned toward Arex, who was coughing. Janiece came over and held his back.

"Are you okay?"

"I can't believe that with the file you have and your knowledge of my existence you still don't have enough evidence to stop another transformation from happening."

"There are several reasons why we can't do anything about this. The reason would be that I obtained the file after it was stolen. I'm liable to be prosecuted for theft by receiving. Not only that, but you are Sandlak's creation. No judge is going to accept your testimony without evidence to back it up. In also couldn't hurt to find out who you were before your transformation. On top of all of that, there is the possible involvement of the American military. There's the question of our word going up against theirs. They are the military power of the entire nation. Nobody is going to believe a small group of people it doesn't matter if they're right."

"But if they are doing something illegal, or allowing something wrong to be done, shouldn't they be stopped?"

"You've been created in the wrong place at the wrong time," stated Jainece.

"What do you mean?"

"If there's one thing people wish to avoid these days, it's a scandal. If BIOGENCORP is exposed, then it will create a domino effect where the Pentagon and everyone else higher up in the nation's political circle will do their best to avoid being caught up with them. For all we know, even the President could be involved in this project. The international reprocutions of the scandal would tear, not only the nation, but the entire world apart. The trick here would be to expose the project and make sure everyone knows what you were sent here for without implicating anybody specific besides Patrick Sandlak."

"Then let's tell everyone. Let's make sure that they see that. And maybe even make Sandlak think that I did what I came here for so that he will show himself. He told me that he would come and fine me in the abandoned apartment once he heard about your murder."

"You mean you think we should stage my death?"

"Yes. What do you think?"

Janiece was suddenly struck with an inspiration. She turned to the two agents.

"Do you think we can do that?"

"It's possible," said Mika Nomura, "we will have to talk to our supervisor, but I think we can pull that plan off."

Chapter 6

Sunday, November 1ˢᵗ, 1998, 5:30 PM
BIOGENCORP Laboratories

Working for BIOGENCORP started off as a dream for Daisy Carter, but it had quickly turned into a living nightmare. Ever since she got her hands on the file describing the A.R.EX. project, she hadn't been able to work properly. She had become afraid of the place where she worked. How could she continue her medical research there while keeping in mind that it was really being used as a front to cover up for something bigger, more bizarre, and definitely dangerous. What was the use of trying to find a cure for a life-threatening disease if her employers' priority is creating giant reptilian monster soldiers for destructive purposes? What made things even worse was the knowledge that the project was being started and implemented down the hall from where she was working. Daisy actually had to walk past the sealed operating chamber whenever she came and went from work. She officially had enough, it was time for her to look for another job, one that didn't involve genetic manipulation…or corruption.

She was just over halfway through her shift, when she was told by one of her colleagues that someone wanted to talk to her over the phone. It was her husband on the other end of the line.

"Paul! Hey baby, how are you doing?"

"I'd like to warn you about something. Pack up your things once you get back. You're out of here."

"What? Why?"

"Because you're going to Florida with me for the next week, maybe even two."

Daisy laughed with incredible relief. This was the first bit of good news she'd heard in a long time. She felt so lucky to have a husband who was willing to plan a surprise trip to her favorite state behind her back. She was excited at the prospect of relaxing for a few days with him and leaving this god-forsaken company behind for good.

"It's high time for you to quit," said Paul, "Get into a violent fight, steal a beaker full of chemicals, I don't care, as long as you get fired without going to jail. Just get yourself out of there, now."

"Okay, hold on. Let me ask a supervisor for a leave of absence. I'll see you tonight anyway. I love you."

Daisy hung up, a heavy weight having been lifted from her shoulders. All she figured she had to do now, was to tell a supervisor that her husband had won a contest that got them a trip to Florida on very short notice. Since she didn't use up any of her vacation days, she figure she could obtain a leave of absence for a good while. Her only hope, though, was that Paul hadn't bought them the plane tickets just yet.

"That sounded like a happy and romantic conversation."

Stunned, Daisy turned around to see Patrick Sandlak standing at the doorway. She had only seen him twice before, and was told that everyone referred to him as the "Chief". She knew that he was leading most of the important projects, which also meant that he was probably heading the A.R.EX. project. That fact made Daisy less than comfortable around him. She also couldn't help but flinch at the sight of the awful scars that marked his face, which gave him a sinister look, despite the seemingly mild disposition that could be seen from his face.

"I'm sorry," he said, "I didn't mean to scare you. I couldn't help but overhearing your phone chat with someone. Who was that, by the way?"

"That was my husband. He won a contest for a trip to Florida, and he wants to take me with him."

"Oh? And when is this trip to take place?"

"Three days from now. It's such short notice, so I doubt I'll be able to go."

She knew it was a terrible lie, but it was the only strategy she had to get a leave from work. Besides, she was pretty sure she could put together a letter of resignation by the time she left.

"Well, I don't see why you shouldn't go," Sandlak replied, "Unless, of course you've taken your vacation time, already."

Daisy's eyes lit up.

"Don't worry, I haven't. Thank you very much, Chief."

"No problem. Just don't forget to send me a postcard."

Even tough she had just had a normal conversation with the Chief, Daisy was glad to be rid of him, even though she still had three hours to go in her shift. It was also unsettling to know that Sandlak heard her exchange with her husband. Now she knew she had to leave at all costs.

She finished her shift without any further incident. Daisy felt a little more at ease at that point. The anticipation of leaving left her feeling like she could smell the aroma of her home already. She put her stuff together quickly enough, and headed out taking one last passing glance at the chamber as she neared the stairs. A sound caught her attention as she turned away. It was a muffled noise, perhaps a metallic clang. She had checked the duty roster this morning, so she knew that no one else was supposed to be on the third floor at the time. She pressed her ear against every other doorway nearby and listened for the sound again. The entire corridor was silent. Comforted by the thought that it was probably just her imagination and paranoia playing a nasty trick on her, she drove out of the building through the underground parking.

*　*　*

Daisy was flustered. She had forgotten her mobile phone, and it took her 15 minutes after she had left to realize it. She really didn't want to go back there, but it was essential that she not have someone from the company find her phone and call her to return it to her, or even worse, just steal it.

The only people left in the building at that point were the night shift guard, who sat at the lobby, and the custodian. Daisy made her way through the darkened corridor, and entered her office.

She opened the light of her laboratory, and searched her desk and the surrounding area thoroughly. Despite her best efforts, though, she couldn't find her phone anywhere.

"Looking for this?"

Daisy froze. The voice had come from behind her. It sounded somewhat familiar, but it sounded strange because it had a raspy quality to it that made it unrecognizable. It sounded as if someone had taken a rusty cheese grater and rubbed it against the inside of his throat.

Daisy slowly turned around, and found herself facing a monster. It was one of those reptile soldier things, a black-skinned being with yellow slashes across its hide. Pepper hair had grown in an unkempt mane on the top and back of its head.

The thing held her cell phone in its left hand. The phone had been turned on and a phone call had been placed to Janiece. Daisy could hear her voice calling out to her.:

"Hello? Daisy? Where are you?"

The reptile snarled, growling the name "Janiece Ryder. It's interesting how you know her."

Before Daisy could act, she was taken and thrown against the wall. As she recovered, she tried calling for help, but the thing was too fast for her. Her screams were immediately drowned out...in her own blood. Her attacker had slit her throat open with its bare claws.

Her hand went to her open throat. Blood was spilling uncontrollably. Daisy soon felt weak as she stumbled on her knees. All the while, she heard Janiece screaming her name, wondering what had happened.

Her attacker grabbed her throat, closing its hand on her wound and putting pressure on it, strangling her. It was clearly trying to prolong her suffering. She felt her life leaving her, her energy gone. All she could do was stare at the monster as it held the phone to the side of its head and said.:

"Beware, because you're next."

As Daisy's body went limp and lifeless, her attacker dropped her phone and crushed it with its bare foot.

* * *

Janiece was shocked as her line with Daisy went dead. Her best friend had just been attacked and was now surely dead. Everybody else was standing in her living room waiting to know what had happened.

"She's dead, I think," she said after a few seconds, "She was attacked while she was trying to call me."

Arex looked at her intently.

"Did she tell you who it was?"

"I don't know who it was, but I heard his voice. It was another A.R.EX. soldier, I'm sure of it."

The voice. It had a raspy quality to it, like Arex, but it lacked Arex's gentler tone of voice. Daisy's killer had a harsh, brutal voice.

"He said I was next. He's coming after me."

"That can only mean one thing," said Mike Scatchard the male FBI agent, "it means that Chief Sandlak might be coming along quite nicely with his massive science project. We've already run out of time, and we just can't catch up to him."

"Wait," said Arex, "how wouldn't he wait for me to get back? And furthermore, wouldn't he attract attention by creating another reptile? And now what will happen to the plan to draw him out?"

"We have to go on as we planned," said Agent Scatchard, "He knows that the law is on his side, but not for long, looking at what just happened to one of his employees. We're not supposed to know she's dead, so we proceed as planned without looking for miss Carter's body until after Sandlak is in custody. Then, after he is interrogated, we can search BIOGENCORP for the body and any other evidence we may find to incriminate Sandlak and any accomplices he might have."

"What about Janiece? Her life is in danger, now."

"We will put her in the F.B.I.'s witness protection program. She will have to come with us to a safe house and live there until we apprehend Sandlak. Our supervisor will arrive shortly. It's important that we set everything up just right."

* * *

7:00 PM
Janiece Ryder's apartment

Corey Rodgers couldn't believe his eyes when he first saw Arex. He also couldn't believe that a talking reptile could hold its own in a normal conversation, or actually seem just as intelligent as any human being. He liked Arex right away, despite being a little afraid of him at first.

He thought Agent Nomura had lost her mind when she told him what had happened earlier on. He wanted her to use force and apprehend the giant reptile at all costs. He realized now that it could have been a huge mistake.

His agents had credited Arex with the idea of drawing Patrick Sandlak out. It had merit, although it was possible that it could backfire now that it was likely Sandlak knew Arex wasn't going to kill Janiece Ryder.

Another cloud over all of their heads was the death of Daisy Carter, Janiece's best friend and the one responsible for getting them the A.R.EX. project file in the first place.

Rodgers had begun to set up a news broadcast of Janiece's death. He would, however, keep the circumstances of her death from the media. The newscast would run for two days starting at ten o'clock the same evening. He hoped it would get Sandlak's attention and that he would come to the abandoned apartment building to pick up as was originally planned. Once that happened, he would arrested and interrogated. It was instrumental that Sandlak be taken into custody, because he was their only link to finding out more about the project.

As for Janiece and Jason Meyers, they would be escorted to a safe house until the dust settled.

*   *   *

1 hour later,
Safe house, New York State

Janiece was escorted to the safe house a couple of hours before the news story of her death was set to broadcast. The place was large, a two-story house, but the lack of open windows made it feel very closed off. She was told that agents were always going to be there on watch. Nobody would be able to come in or out of there without the agents knowing about it. They were monitoring everything happening inside and around the perimeter of the building with security cameras set up at every access point.

They were whisked away before any of them had time to talk to the Simons about Kip knowing about Arex's existence. The F.B.I. felt it was best not to have them worry by arriving at their apartment. Janiece hoped Kip would be able to hold his tongue until Arex was shown off the right way. She also knew it was best for their family not to get involved in this matter, since it might put them in serious danger.

There was also a new problem coming up: Mika Nomura had told her privately that Patrick Sandlak was the one who had extradited Rick Meyers and brought him to Albany as an A.R.EX. "volunteer." Jason's father was unknowingly awaiting a transformation into a talking killer reptile. For all she knew, it had probably already happened, and he was awaiting his first task as an A.R.EX. soldier.

All the while, Jason was worried about Arex's well-being.

"Do you think he's going to be okay?"

"Of course, sweetie. You've seen him, he can definitely take care of himself if he needs to. He's tougher than even he knows."

"I hope so. He's a really cool guy."

"He's really brave," Janiece agreed, "he doesn't know it, but we owe him our lives. It's too bad he probably thinks he's the one who put them in danger."

It made her wonder what would happen to him after this mess was over. Would he be sent to prison and serve his former self's sentence? What if he wasn't? Would he actually be able to be integrated into society, a society which can hold a lot of prejudice towards people who don't fit in what was considered the norm?

In that sense, she felt a connection with Arex. It was a challenge for her to get to where she was, not only because of her gender, but also because she was African-American. She had to climb her way out of the preconceptions and into her current position. The only thing she could do now, was wait and gauge the public's reaction toward Arex's existence, and hope it would be a favorable one.

* * *

The next day, 10:06 AM
Albany, New York

Patrick Sandlak was sitting at home that afternoon. He was feeling pretty confident now that he was one step closer to achieving his goals. Now all he had to do was tie up some more loose ends, and then he could make sure his project would come to fruition. He also realized that he couldn't afford to make any mistakes at this point. Even though he wasn't home-free, so to speak, he felt that there was nothing that could stop him now. He was going to wait until dusk, and find Arex and Janiece Ryder, who were . For the moment, he settled himself in his living room, watching TV to pass the time.

An hour later, he made himself a sandwich as the 12 o'clock news were showing. As he was eating in the kitchen, he heard the headlines. One of those headlines, was about a murder that occurred in an apartment building in New York City. His curiosity piqued, he waited and watched for that story to show in detail.

"A mysterious tragedy has occurred in an apartment complex in New York City. Janiece Ryder, 27, was found murdered in her home. Miss Ryder was an attorney at law for Henry's Law Firm. Her body was found brutally beaten and slashed to death yesterday. There are no clear suspects, but the F.B.I. has taken over the investigation in earnest. Details will be available as they come. Janiece Ryder was best known as the attorney who represented Erickson Meyers during his murder trial. Erickson Meyers' eight-year-old son, Jason, was in the apartment during the attack, but thankfully, was asleep, and was never discovered."

Sandlak smiled maliciously. The story was a trap set to bait him, that much was clear. The F.B.I., and Sandlak's own creation were baiting him in order to draw him out. Well, he was going to take the bait, but they were the ones in for the surprise of their life once he got there.

Chapter 7

Monday, November 2ⁿᵈ, 1998, 9:27 PM
Abandoned apartment, New York City

Arex had almost already forgotten where to find the old, empty apartment building. He really hoped he would never have to go back there. Coming back there and seeing, smelling breathing everything inside gave him nausea. That was bad enough, but his escort, Mike Scatchard, apparently thought it was a good idea to pass the time by commenting on everything Arex already knew was foul about the building.

The F.B.I. had worked for hours, setting up surveillance cameras in and around the apartment before they arrived. Arex was impressed at how hard it was to find the cameras without one of the agents pointing them out to him. Mike also carried a device with him called a radio that would allow them to communicate with the agents located in a van nearby.

"You know, Mika told me this guy Sandlak has some scars on his face that look like claw marks. How bad are they?"

"I wouldn't know how to answer that. They are the only scars I've ever seen, so I can't compare them to any other. In fact, if Sandlak hadn't told me so himself, I would have told you that they were simply a part of his skin."

"It's gotta be tough. I mean having to re-learn everything that you're supposed to know already."

"It's not that bad. There are some things I recognize, though I can't tell you how or why. I don't feel like I'm missing anything from my former life. Then again, I don't even remember ever having a former life."

"You're going to have a very hard time learning everything you don't know about the world you live in. People will just assume that you'll be able to hit your marks and magically figure everything out right away. Doesn't that bother you?"

"Maybe a little, but there's nothing I can do about it. If you want to know, there is a part of me that feels like I want to prove myself to people and show them that I can live in this society."

Arex saw Mike taking his palm to his face in what seemed like exasperation.

"You're way too good to be true. In our line of work, that's suspicious."

"Why do you say that?"

"Because you don't get it. Here, in this society, people just don't act like you, especially not when they're your age. They're not this innocent, this helpful, or this nice. It's not natural, and it makes people think you're constantly up to something.."

"What do you mean?"

"I've only known you for about a day or so, and I've never seen you angry. It's like you're the representation, the very symbol of kindness. You have a gentile heart, and it just doesn't fit with the way you look. I know, it's not right for me to be judging your character in this way, but still, you're a little weird."

"So what you're saying is, I have to act in a different manner? Why should I live according to what other people think I should do and say? Isn't that just as unnatural?"

Arex suddenly felt uncomfortable with being so...unique.

There was nobody else out in the world who could relate to the way he was feeling.

"Agent Scatchard?"

"Call me Mike."

"Alright, Mike. Should I be acting a certain way? What should I be like, according to you?"

"Well, from what someone like me has read, an anthropomorphic reptile such as yourself shouldn't care about other people, have a very angry disposition, and have a very audible lisp."

"What's a lisp?"

"A hissing sound. It makes one slur his S's."

"Do I really have to be that way? It sounds stupid and annoying."

"You're right, it's actually just a comic book stereotype. And I tend to sound like a complete idiot sometimes when I make a reference to something I read from one. People say that my inner geek is either my most endearing, or my most annoying feature. You know what? Just forget everything I said about your behavior. You're great the way you are, so just stay that way."

"Did you think I was a monster when we first met? Were you afraid of me?"

"Oh definitely. You look pretty scary."

"What do you think of me now?"

"I think you're pretty cool. And I also think that Janiece might have some feelings for you."

"What do you mean by that?"

"I mean romance."

"Romance? With me?"

"Why not?"

"Because I'm not human. And Janiece is a little afraid of me. I also suspect that she thinks I'm not smart. Not to mention the fact that I was sent here to kill her. She hasn't forgotten about that, how can she? Besides, she doesn't trust me. You heard what she said in front of everybody."

"That was her maternal instincts kicking in. She was afraid that Jason would be in danger. Think about it this way: If you weren't sent here to kill her, someone else would, and maybe then she wouldn't be alive today. And if you didn't exist and she would be killed, you two wouldn't have met in the first place. Do you see? It's a good thing you both met."

"I suppose you're right," said Arex, though he wasn't too convinced by Mike's words.

Night had fallen a couple of hours earlier. The pair waited, wondering whether or not Sandlak had seen the newscast, and if and/or when he would come. To pass the time, Mike began teaching Arex how to play with cards. The silence of the surrounding area was unbearable and only broken by the occasional car passing by. From the window in the empty bedroom, Arex could see only the street in front of the building, and not the alleyway. Everything else was blocked from their view, but could be seen by the agents in the van.

Suddenly, the lights in the building went out. Mike's radio gave him a signal.

"Yes?"

"Be advised, there is a car slowing down in the vicinity of the building. We also have to warn you that the cameras are down."

"What's happening out there?"

"Somebody cut the power outside of the building. We're coming to your location, but it will take some time to arrive. If Sandlak arrives, you will have to apprehend him alone."

"Roger that."

He closed the radio and turned to Arex, whispering.

"Looks like Sandlak has a friend in the electric company. Just relax, the other agents are on their way. I'm getting into position."

"Understood."

Mike hid himself in the small bedroom, while Arex stood in the living room and waited, staring at the door. His stomach in knots, he listened as someone walked up the stairs and eventually came to a halt and knocked hard on the door.

Arex breathed in hard. His pulse racing, he slowly walked to the door. When he opened it, he was shaken right through to his core. His visitor wasn't human, it was another A.R.EX. reptile.

This reptile was dressed mostly in black with a leather jacket and jogging pants, and a green t-shirt. His hair was graying, and his eyes were a clear grey. Arex guessed that the human used was older than he was.

"Fancy meeting you here, traitor," the newcomer rasped.

Traitor? Arex had always felt like he was the one who was betrayed. He was created from someone else, his memories erased. On top of that, he had almost killed someone on false orders.

"The only traitor I know is Patrick Sandlak," said Arex.

As he said it, something about the face of the other reptile struck him. There, on the left side of his face, were three scars barely visible on the black hide.

"You… you're Patrick Sandlak."

"Took you long enough to figure it out. Yes, it's me."

"Are you insane? Why did you do this to yourself?"

"Well, you kind of force my hand when you betrayed me, your creator."

"You are not my creator, you're a monster, a crazed scientist."

"I may be insane, but you owe me your very existence, and you have a funny way of showing your gratitude."

"You expect me to show you gratitude? For what? Changing my body, erasing my memory and abandoning me in this strange world I no nothing about? Should I really feel grateful for that?"

"If it weren't for me, you'd be rotting from the inside out in a prison."

"But you took me from that prison, stole my very self from me, and then ordered me to kill an innocent person."

"It seems I should have trained you in the art of killing. You wouldn't be such a bleeding heart. Compassion, honesty, love, they have no place in this world."

"I can't believe what I just heard. The art of killing? Do you really believe that taking someone's life can be a beautiful thing?"

"It is when it's for the right reason. For example, I will enjoy it when I paint the floor with your blood."

"You're disgusting. Just because you've never felt love from other people, it doesn't mean you should make it your life's work to destroy other people and end their lives simply because they don't agree with your way of thinking. I may not have many memories, but I know that much."

"Do you really think I hated being human? I had a decent family. I was always a proud father."

"Then why are you doing this? I could have someone's father, husband, or even brother."

"And you were also Erickson Meyers, the convicted criminal who killed an entire family out of revenge. No one cares about you. As far as I know, I did you a favor."

That was all Arex could take. He took Sandlak and pushed him up against the wall.

"How dare you?! Jason loved his father. He thinks about him all the time. Janiece never stopped believing in his innocence..."

"...Maybe she just told you that because she knew who you were all along. How long did she beg before you finally spare her life?!"

"Arex! Let him go, man. He's just trying to get under your skin. If you fall for it, he dies winning."

115

Arex, still holding Sandlak, turned to see Mike, who had a hand to his gun.

"Yes, Arex listen to the agent," Sandlak hissed, "be a good little boy and let me go before anybody thinks even less of you."

Arex fought with himself for a few second while he let Sandlak go. The latter was breathing heavily. Arex pondered: Should he hold on a little more? Was Sandlak really thinking about giving up, and submitting to the F.B.I.'s interrogation? What if he tried to run? Would Arex be fast enough to catch him? What about the other F.B.I. agents, the one surveying the whole scene? When would they intervene, if ever at all?

"Come on, Sandlak," said Mike, "hands in the air. You're under arrest for the attempted murder of Janiece Ryder, the murder of Daisy Carter, and the illegal extradition of Erickson Meyers."

Sandlak turned to the side, still breathing hard. As he started putting his hands up, he spun around , using his tail to whip both Mika and Arex so hard, they were thrown to the floor. Mike, whom the tail caught in the chest, hit the bedroom door frame before collapsing on his side.

Arex quickly recovered from his blow. He lunged forward, catching Sandlak on his left, tripping him and then pinning him down. His opponent was quick, kicking him the ribs, pushing Arex away and to the side.

Arex fell to the right, pain searing through his ribs. He put his hand to his flank, grunting as he tried to pull himself up. He had just managed to stand up, when Sandlak jumped on his back weighed him down. On the defensive, Arex felt he had roll over in order to gain the upper hand, but Sandlak had him pinned and was throwing punch after punch, leaving his opponent incapacitated. Trying to respond, Arex slapped Sandlak's arms away from him, grabbed his t-shirt, and rolled him over. As he tried to pin Sandlak's arms to his sides, his foe started clawing at him, the nails biting into his skin. Being unable to bear the pain much longer, Arex punched Sandlak, cracking his jaw.

Sandlak recovered fast, got his hands free, and punched Arex in the same ribs he'd hurt before. Arex stumbled to the side, pain blurring his vision. Sandlak took the chance, tackled Arex, and rammed him into the wooden desk, shattering it.

Fear gripped Arex. He wasn't certain he'd be able to stop Arex on his own. He looked up, and saw Sandlak looming over him. Arex had no will to fight anymore, he was in pain and fatigued.

"It's over," said Sandlak. "Say goodbye to your short life."

BANG!

A loud popping sound was heard behind them. Sandlak jerked up as something seemed to him in the back. Arex nudged himself sideways. Looking behind Sandlak, he saw Mike, who was on his knees, holding a smoking pistol in his hands. Sandlak was now clutching his chest, where a dark red stain was growing on it.

Sandlak stumbled to his knees, his breathing getting more and more labored. Mike, still holding his gun and his ribcage, was now calling for an ambulance on his radio. People running could be heard outside.

"If you check the dumpster beside our building, you will find the body of Daisy Carter."

That statement took Arex by surprise. It meant that Daisy Carter was, in fact, dead, and that Sandlak was likely the one who killed her, but why was he saying that now of all times? Could they even trust what he just told them?

"My family was mostly military. I lost my father, my-my brother," he rasped, "my sons, my wife. I-I just couldn't handle it any more. I figured low-life criminals wouldn't be missed. D-D-Did Jason really...love his father that much?"

"He never stopped believing in his innocence," Arex replied.

"Good. That's the way it should be."

Arex struggled to his feet, then edged his way to his wounded creator. If he really had to bury his entire family, then Sandlak had the right to a little empathy. How does it feel when a father outlives his son because of a war?

Sandlak was now fumbling inside his pocket, still breathing harshly, blood still pouring from his wound. Arex saw him taking a shiny red object out.

Before anybody else could react, Sandlak made a knife appear from the object and plunged it his throat. They could only watch as he turned the knife on its side, while it was still in his neck. Finally, with a last effort, Sandlak took the knife out. As blood sprayed heavily on the floor, the body slumped down, limp.

He's dead. Arex couldn't believe what just happened. Someone just died right in front of his eyes. His mind went blurry, barely registering Mike's frantic voice over the radio. Why would someone choose to end his or her life, especially in such a brutal manner?

Mike bent down and put his fingers on Sandlak's throat.

"Suspect is dead. I repeat, suspect is dead. He just stuck a Swiss Army knife in his neck."

Arex felt Mike's hand on his shoulder, taking his mind away from the body.

"An ambulance is on the way," Mike told him, "we should get ourselves stitched up. You're bleeding."

Arex looked down and found several cuts and bruises from his fight. He didn't really care about his injuries, though. One question was still on his mind.

"Do you think he was telling the truth?"

"What?"

"Was he telling the truth? About me, and Janiece's friend?"

"Who knows? Who knows if he even had a family, much less lost one. You can't trust a criminal."

"You mean a criminal like me?"

Mike was about to answer, but kept quiet, and Arex knew why. The question of Arex's identity was never a huge problem, but this was personal. Jason was in Janiece's care, and he might also be his son, and that fact would completely change the dynamics of the relationship between them.

He took one last look at the body which now laid on the floor. Did he hate Sandlak for what had happened to him before and after his creation? Not really. He was comfortable with who he was now, did he really want to change back? That was why he didn't hate Sandlak.

It was only then that he started to feel the smarting pain in his body. The cuts weren't very deep, but there were so many of them, they slowed him down considerably. At least one thing was certain, it was officially the last time he needed to be in that abandoned apartment building.

Chapter 8

Janiece was going through a range of emotions as she arrived at the hospital. She had been told by the F.B.I. that her friend Daisy was, in fact, dead. She also learned that Patrick Sandlak had chosen to transform himself into a reptile so he could kill both her and Arex. Thankfully both Arex and F.B.I. agent Mike Scatchard weren't that seriously injured. As for Janiece, she had to contend with emotions that were simmering inside of her. She felt anger at Patrick Sandlak for the fact that he killed her best friend. She felt grief that Daisy was gone, and there was no bringing her back. There was a considerable amount of sadness, because this all happened because of sick man's dream. On a positive note, though, she was relieved to hear that Arex was still alive. She couldn't believe it when Mika Nomura told Arex might have once been Rick Meyers. It frightened her a bit, when she thought about what might've happened had Arex not decided to be on her side. Then she, along with Daisy would be frozen in a morgue, and Sandlak would still be alive.

Jason was very excited, something Janiece hadn't seen. She hadn't told him about Arex, but Jason was falling in love with the guy anyway. She wondered whether or not he'd still feel that way if he knew the truth.

They were escorted by F.B.I. agents wherever they went, and Janiece had mixed feelings about that. She felt safe, but also a little annoyed. It was having one's grandmother hold one's hand just to cross the street. The head of the Criminal Investigation Division, Corey Rodgers.

When they arrived at the hospital, they were led to the third floor. After crossing a small hallway, they found their ward. Doctor Denis Kelly greeted them there.

"They were in pretty bad shape when they arrived," Dr. Kelly explained, "Some of Mr. Scatchard's lower ribs were slightly fractured and are causing him great discomfort and pain. He will have to remain in the hospital for at least a week, and have those bandages on for around two months. As for the...uh...other gentleman, his wounds have already started to heal. I have to say I've never had to deal with this sort of thing before."

Janiece nearly gagged. The "other" gentleman? This sort of "thing"? Dr. Kelly was talking about Arex like he was some sort of animal. She had half a mind to chastise him for that. On second thought, though, she realized that that was exactly how she first reacted to Arex, thinking of him more as an object rather than an actual person. She resigned herself to biting her tongue and waiting for Dr. Kelly to finish his diagnosis.

"I have noticed, however, that he seems to have a concussion. I will have to take an X-Ray to be sure," said the doctor.

"Why do you think he has a concussion?"

"He doesn't know today's date, the year, or the name of the president..."

"Hold on," she intervened. "Hasn't anybody told you? He wouldn't know these things anyway. His memories have been erased."

Dr. Kelly double-checked Arex's file on his clipboard.

"Oh, I'm sorry. I didn't know. It's not written here. I guess nobody in the ambulance bothered to ask him."

"I'm not the one you should be apologizing to, but it's okay. I can imagine, though, that he was a little puzzled when you asked him these questions. Anyway, what are the details of his condition?"

"Stable. Both of them are conscious but he's already able to move around without reopening his wounds and bleeding profusely. There are a lot of bandaged scars, but at this point, the bandages might be more of a bother than anything else. For all I really know, he can probably take them off tomorrow, if he continues to heal this way. I can probably release him tonight without too much worry."

"Good. Thank you for your assessment. Oh, and, by the way, his name is Arex."

They walked around the flustered doctor, and got to the bed where Arex was lying down. Mike Scatchard was on the bed next to him. For a while, she couldn't tell which one of them was in worse shape. Arex had what looked like thirty bandages of all sizes covering his body. Despite that, though, he sat up on the bed when he saw them, looking at them. She tried to guess his mindset at this point, and speculated that he was happy to see them. She noticed that when his eyes turned toward Jason, his head bowed. Was it shame? For what? What exactly had Sandlak told him? She wouldn't know unless the F.B.I. released the tape recording of that conversation to her.

"How are you feeling?"

"I'm alright," he replied, "Mike told me these bandages make me look like a zebra. Whatever that is."

Of course. How could he possibly know what a zebra is? He doesn't know anything about this planet. It was easy for Janiece to forget that Arex was somewhat clueless about many things that would be common knowledge to the average human being. She realized that it was going to take some serious dedication to educate a grown amnesic adult. He would probably have to take classes in order to obtain his grade, junior high, and high school diplomas, and maybe more, depending on what he wanted to do in life. *Wait a minute, slow down there, brain. He's not there, yet. On thing at a time.* Right now, the important was getting a case together against BIOGENCORP. The lawyer in her decided that now was time to make it a priority.

"You're both going to have to write down a statement about what happened," said Janiece, "unless you'd rather make a voice recording."

"I think I'll try writing it," Arex replied.

Janiece raised her eyebrows. She doubted that Patrick Sandlak had let Arex walk away with every one of Rick's abilities. Then again, the Mind Shifter computer was only created for the purpose of erasing one's personal memories. She decided she would test that thought. She reached into her purse.

"Fine," she said, "here's a pen, and a notepad. Write the first thing that comes to your mind."

"Thank you."

He took the pen and pad. Janiece's eyes went wide. Seemingly without even thinking, Arex put the pen in his left hand, and started to write. He handed the pad over to Janiece. It read "Do you think it's true?"

"I know what you mean, and I'm not sure. One thing is for sure, he was right-handed. You're not."

As Arex was going to speak, Janiece heard Corey Rodgers walking briskly toward them.

"It's a media circus out there. There are news reporters, camera crews, vans, and a huge crowd. Everyone wants to see the talking reptile."

Janiece sighed.

"This isn't a good time," she said, "please, tell them he's in no condition to be talking to the media."

"Wait a minute," Arex interjected, "I thought we had established that keeping me a secret wasn't a good idea."

"It's not keeping you a secret per say, rather, letting you recover. Besides, you seem to need a press agent."

"A lawyer that can handle the media for you up to a certain extent."

Arex nodded his understanding, then added.:

"Aren't you a lawyer?"

"Are you asking me to be your press agent, Mr. Arex?"

Arex gave a throaty chuckle. Janiece figured that it was much against his nature to laugh. He then stood straight up, put one hand behind his back, used the other hand to clear his throat, then stated.:

"Yes, absolutely. Miss Ryder, will you please talk to the press on my behalf and tell them that I will address them when I feel the time is right."

Everyone in the ward Janiece knew erupted in laughter as they heard his voice trying to convey over-the-top businessman mannerisms he so obviously must have seen on TV. Mike, whose ribs couldn't handle all that laughter, quickly winced in pain, but still kept a smile on his face.

"Good one Arex," said Jason.

"Thank you. I was just trying to feel better, myself."

"Well, you sure made us feel better" said Janiece.

Corey Rodgers made a whistling noise, trying to get everyone's attention.

"On a more serious note, Arex, we have to ask you to come with us to Albany. We need someone who knows BIOGENCORP headquarters better than we do, to escort us to where you were created and held."

"But I don't know where I was created," Arex explained, "I doubt the transformation took place in the bedroom I woke up in."

"Nevertheless, you do know the place to a certain extent. Can you handle going there again?"

Janiece watched Arex hesitate before finally saying.: "Yes."

"Good," said Rodgers, "We'll leave as soon as miss Ryder gets the media out of here."

Chapter 9

It had been almost two weeks since Mark Reeves was last at work. Being in the Bahamas with his family really helped to clear his mind up. He did have some insecurities about leaving the company in Patrick Sandlak's hands, but it turned out not to be problem. As far as he could tell, the company was running smoothly. So smoothly, in fact that Sandlak had apparently taken the day off. Reeves thought it was a good idea, seeing as Sandlak had to manage the entire company, while at the same time, working his normal shifts.

Feeling elated, Reeves took a look at the journal he told Sandlak to write while he was away. Sandlak had managed to extradite Erickson Meyers from prison, the latter was now in a halfway house in New York City, awaiting the transformation. Sandlak also had the necessary documents for the next 14 volunteers, as well as the vouchers for the funding of the A.R.EX. project spanning the expenses for the next three months, which included the construction of a training center and housing facilities, as well the necessary staff to construct and man the buildings. On another note, the forensics and research teams were operating at peak efficiency.

Everything seemed to be falling in place perfectly, it was almost too good to be true. The only black mark in the report was the firing of Daisy Carter. Sandlak wrote that she wasn't working to the best of her ability, often wasting her time on the clock. Still, without her absence, the research team was meeting its schedule every day, so it was her loss she was fired, not theirs.

Reeves decided to make a round of the building, going through every nook and cranny, practically trying to find something wrong that might have happened while he was away. He was going to gauge the staff's morale as well as their level of fatigue.

Everyone looked to be in high spirits, which was a good sign. Nothing seemed out of place, except for Daisy Carter's office. Nobody had seen her clear out her things, and yet they were all gone. Not only that, but her office smelled of cleaning products and bleach. *Maybe someone was a little pissed from getting fired*, Reeves thought. Some kind of incident must've happened the day before. It looked like something went wrong during his leave after all.

He got back to his office to read the documents Sandlak left on his desk, when his office phone rang.

"Hello?"

"Sir, you better come see this," said a security guard from the lobby. "There are about a dozen or so F.B.I. agents here and they wish to search the premises."

What?!

"Do not let them anywhere near the other floors. I'll be right there."

Surely there must've been some mistake. Why would the F.B.I. want to search his company's building. They'd done nothing wrong as far as he knew.

He made his way down to the first floor lobby. When he arrived, there were several F.B.I. agents amassed near the doors. What shocked Reeves was seeing what looked like an

A.R.EX. soldier among them. That was impossible, since the next test wasn't supposed to happen until he got back. That alone was surprising enough, but it also looked like it had just come back from battle.

Reeves was confused until he saw one of the agents. It was Sora Takahashi. She was working for the F.B.I.? Her entire identity was probably false. He wondered what she had found in such a limited amount of time with them.

When Miss Takahashi (if that was even her real name) saw him, she turned to the reptile and pointed at him. Words were exchanged and the reptile shook his head. Reeves then watched helplessly as a few agents converged on him.

"Sir," said one of the agents, "we have a search warrant for the premises."

"May I ask what you might be looking for?"

"Evidence. It is my duty to inform you that the body of one of your employees was found in the garbage dumpster next to your building."

"What? Whose body?"

"Daisy Carter."

"Miss Carter? She was fired two days ago."

"Actually, Dr. Sandlak transformed himself into a reptile, attacked and killed her in cold blood. We are going to search for the evidence to support that conclusion."

What started off as a perfect day, was fast going downhill. Now he found himself in the midst of an F.B.I. investigation. Why was Daisy Carter murdered, and did Patrick Sandlak have anything to do with it?

"Before we continue," said the agent, "I would also like to inform you that according to our witness here," he pointed toward the reptile, "Patrick Sandlak wanted him to kill miss Janiece Ryder. Dr. Sandlak himself admitted to murdering Daisy Carter."

"If he did those things, then I can obviously allow you to search his office, but not the rest of the building."

"Our warrant covers the entire building. You can't keep us from any room."

*   *   *

As the F.B.I. searched the building, Reeves had to escort their supervisor, Corey Rodgers, and answer all of his questions. The entire company was put on hold while the F.B.I. invasion continued.

"Where is the operation chamber?"

"The door is on the third floor, at the end of the corridor."

"We have here a receipt for renovations done. We called up the contractor, and he said that he gutted the third floor ceiling, and the fourth floor...floor."

"Yes. We need the extra space for the main computer."

"How can you have a computer that's over eight feet tall? This isn't 1950. Show me the chamber."

Chapter 10

Monday, November 2ⁿᵈ, 1998, 2:47 PM
Janiece Ryder's apartment

As the F.B.I. was searching BIOGENCORP Laboratories, Janiece had decided to look into what she could piece together. Whenever she worked on a case, she wanted to create a timeline. What she couldn't really understand was why Rick Meyers was chosen for the transformation. Rick hadn't received any military training. Nothing in his file suggested that he could be an efficient soldier. The only thing that might have made him a fighter was six years spent learning Aikido, obtaining a 3rd level black belt. That was it. What a waste.

And now she had to make sense of the events that transpired. She made notes, writing down everything. She organized a timeline, figuring it would help put things in perspective and let her piece together everything that happened and why.

A.R.EX. Project: Chain of events.

1. *March 1997:BIOGENCORP Laboratories is hired by the Pentagon (or so it seemed, that fact remains unclear) to create a deadly new weapon, that would*

be unique in every aspect, while also complying with laws banning the development of nuclear weaponry. The budget for the project is set at just over a billion dollars in research and development for the project alone.

2. *April: Despite my best efforts, Erickson Meyers is convicted of murder, and sentenced to 25 years in prison.*

3. *October 26th: Patrick Sandlak arrives at Bare Hill and extradites Rick Meyers using a document showing my signature, which was forged (who his source was is currently unknown, but I suspect it is one of my colleagues. It would probably be that same person who later informed Sandlak that I had the A.R.EX. File in my possession.)*

4. *October 27th: Daisy discovers the A.R.EX. Files while doing a routine maintenance checkup on BIOGENCORP's computers. She downloads the file and faxes it to me. Patrick Sandlak finds out that I know about A.R.EX. and probably decides that it's time for Rick to go through the transformation. Arex wakes up on the 29th, a completely different person from Rick, both inside and out.*

5. *October 31st: After being thoroughly tested, Arex is dropped off in the abandoned apartment building a few block from my complex. He's given the instruction to kill me as part of his first mission as a solider. That same night, he arrives at my apartment.*

As she wrote that part, she felt her forearm, where Arex had accidentally scratched her.

But he doesn't kill me. Instead, he warned me of the danger I was in. He saved my life.

Janiece felt an incredible feeling of happiness and relief. She owed him her life. She had no right in her mind to doubt him and his intentions. Putting that thought aside for now, she continued with her next section. Her own little private investigation.

Questions that need answering.

1. *Out of the many criminals held in Bare Hill alone, why was Rick Meyers chosen over everyone else?*

Reason1: Convenience.
My signature was forged, presumably by one of my colleagues. Every one of them already knew how vocal I was in believing in Rick's innocence. It would easy for everyone to point the finger at me when the time was right.
Reason 2: Experimentation.
Rick was mute, that was pretty much known in the firm. Sandlak may have also had half a mind to use the A.R.EX. serum and promote it as a medical drug. It doesn't matter at this point, since Sandlak seems to have taken the secret of the composition of the serum with him to the grave.

2. *Who is the one who forged my signature?*

It has to be one of my colleagues. One who would have access to my documents, anything with my signature on it. That same person found out that Daisy had sent me the fax with A.R.EX. file on it. It has to be a lawyer in order to have his or her sign the document. That person would likely have Patrick Sandlak as a client.

She called Joe Henry.
"Hello?"

"I think I have something figured out. The person who forged my signature might have Patrick Sandlak as a client. He or she is one of us. Can you find me that person?"

She hung up. In the meantime, she was still waiting for Arex to come out of the shower wearing the new clothes she bought him. She wasn't even sure whether or not the clothes would fit him.

"Are you done?"

"I'm almost finished," Arex called from the bathroom.

As he said that, ripping sounds were heard. Janiece feared that the clothes were too small and were being torn apart.

Arex finally appeared in the living room. He was wearing a white T-shirt and a plaid, long-sleeve shirt on top of it. He also wore a pair of blue jeans that ended around his ankles. He held his pair of sneakers in one hand, and the socks in the other.

"I see you didn't wear the sneakers," she observed.

"I'm sorry," said Arex "but they didn't fit."

"Okay. Here, give them to me."

Arex handed her the sneakers. She took a pair of scissors and created a hole at the toe of each. She did the same with the socks.

"Normally, people would recommend against doing something like this, but I think you can pull this off. Your feet need shoes. Winter is coming soon, and they'll freeze if you keep them bare. With these holes, at least your feet will fit in them."

"But, doesn't this mean I'm ruining the shoes."

"Usually, but then again, the norm never really applied to you."

Arex shrugged and put on his footwear. With the holes in his socks and shoes, his long-nailed toes protruding out.

"See? You can pull this off no problem at all," said Janiece. "And maybe your feet won't sweat as much as some other men's do in their shoes."

"That's a problem?"

"Let's just say I've had experience with men and athlete's foot. It's not an enticing fragrance. Either way, I like it. You look nice."

"Thank You."

To Janiece, it felt important that Arex look as approachable as possible. The only way that was going to happen, was if he'd dress in a casual way. She knew it would help people when they got to know him. If there was one thing she realized, though, it was that Arex could never pull off a tailored suit. The casual clothing also complemented his calm personality, which was a big plus. Janiece smiled when she realized he looked ten years younger than he actually was. The down side to his look was that people may have a hard time taking him seriously.

She noticed Arex was also trying on his new cap. It looked strange because his head's configuration didn't really allow for a cap to fit properly on it. Jason, who was looking from his bedroom door, seemed to noticed that also. Arex turned to him, and asked.:

"How do I look?"

"Uh...you look kind of okay," said Jason, "but the cap makes you look like you're trying to hide your face."

"Well, I don't want to look like I'm trying to hide something."

"Here, let me fix that."

Arex bent down so that Jason could reach his head. Jason then took the cap. Janiece nearly laughed as Arex winced in pain. After taking the cap, Jason had pulled the front end of Arex's mane. Still holding on to it, he then slipped the hair through the cap where the adjustable Velcro strands were joined. *Now this is a good idea*, Janiece thought. With the cap now backwards, Arex's face was now better framed.

The phone rang. Janiece picked it up. It was her boss.

"I've just reviewed our clients' lists. You were right, one of us does have a client in Patrick Sandlak."

"Who?"

"Kirk Hall."

No Way! Suddenly, everything seemed to fall into place in Janiece's mind.

"He's the one who answered when Daisy called my office. He's the one who handled the fax I received. It all makes sense."

"I'll have to have a word with him, and invite the F.B.I. over."

"See you in a week."

Chapter 11

Tuesday, November 3rd, 1998, 4:31 PM
F.B.I. New York City Headquarters

Mika was satisfied with her investigation so far. After having interviewed most of the employees and taken the equipment apart, she was now in the process preparing to interrogate Mark Reeves. She and her colleagues already figured from the interviews that only the senior staff really knew what the A.R.EX. project was about. It was important to figure out whether or not Reeves was involved in the act, or was just a negligent boss. Either way, he was likely to face charges.

Her partner, Mike, was recovering in the hospital, and Patrick Sandlak was dead. It was a shame that nobody would ever know the secret to the A.R.EX. serum, but there was nothing that could be done about that. Dismantling the project was now going to be easy, barring interference from Reeves' sponsors, whoever they were. She doubted all along that the Pentagon would invest billions in such a risky endeavor. Whoever these clients were, they had to be found and exposed. First thing was first, though, and that was interrogating Mark Reeves.

She left her office, and headed two floors down, to the interrogation room where Reeves was held. When she entered, he looked at her intently. She guessed that he probably felt a little duped by her. She sat down laying a file on the table in front of them.

"Just so you know," she started, "my name is really Mika Nomura. I am an experienced field agent for the F.B.I.. I would like to ask you a few questions."

"Why should I answer anything you ask me? I would like to speak to my lawyer."

"You already have everything going against you. Lawyering up would just make you even guiltier."

"Guilty? Of what?"

"Of fraud, forgery, and conspiracy to commit murder. You have a chance to make it go all the way down to criminal negligence."

"But, I don't understand. What happened?"

"How long where you away in the Bahamas? One and half weeks?"

"Yes."

"Well, to me anyway, that now feels like an eternity. So much has happened. So much that you've missed because you felt like going on a little vacation."

"I was just trying to enjoy some time with my family. You can't convict me for that."

"No one blames you for wanting a little R and R, but the timing is a little suspicious. While you were away, Patrick Sandlak was in charge. You already knew he extradited Erickson Meyers from Bare Hill Correctional, but did you know that the documents were forged? Kirk Hall never approached his colleague, Janiece Ryder, about signing the papers. Neither was the judge whose name appears on the document."

"I never knew that. Kirk is someone I knew from Pat. I also heard of his successes, so I figured he played by the rules."

"Unfortunately, you were wrong. Mr. Hall is also under

investigation for corruption. Now, where is Erickson Meyers held?"

"From what I know he's held in a house here in New York."

"Wrong. Meyers is gone, dead. Instead, there's the reptile you saw in the lobby this morning."

"No."

"Yes. No you see the fruits of Dr. Sandlak's labor. An amnesic reptile who was ordered to kill his former lawyer. Your absence has led to an unbelievable chain of events. This is going to change the world and bring some unwanted attention to the American military. Now, it's important to know who your client is."

"That's classified information."

"We will find out. You better hope that you were just as duped as Meyers was when he signed up for this project. Arex, the reptile, is taking you down for your contribution to this mess."

Mika excused herself and left the interrogation room. Corey Rodgers was waiting for her outside in the hall. Rodgers had spent the better part of the afternoon going through BIOGENCORP's financial records.

"Reeves is not budging on the client front. I couldn't get anything out of him. I doubt he even really knows who his clients really were. There's no way the Pentagon could possibly be involved in such a crackpot."

"I agree. In fact, the bank account to which we tracked the funds coming to BIOGENCORP is a Swiss bank account with the name Samuel Berry. There is no Sam Berry in the Pentagon's roster. The account has billions stored in it. I'm speculating, but it might be tied to a foreign power. We may never know who hired them."

Part 3

Aftermath

Chapter 1

Monday, November 9, 1998, 10:01 AM
F.B.I. NYC Headquarters

As he entered the F.B.I. building, Arex felt more than a little nervous. With the cleanliness and order of the hallways and the personnel, Arex felt like an outsider in his casual clothing. Everything and everyone was in shades rather than colors.

Naturally, another thing that made him feel uncomfortable was the stares he was enduring from the staff in the hallway. Obviously, they were warned of his coming, which was probably why nobody ran off, shrieking. There were glares, indifferent glances, shocked faces, and, incredibly, a couple of trusting smiles. It seemed he was a celebrity now, so he had to get used to that.

He entered the conference room behind Janiece. She immediately sat down on one side of the table. Arex was unsure of where to sit down. Janiece urged him to sit next to her. Everyone entered the room one at a time. Arex noticed Mike Scatchard was present, probably hiding his bandaged ribs under his suit. Corey Rodgers arrived last and sat at the end of the table. Arex was told prior that he wasn't to speak until spoken to, a habit he was to pick up before taking the stand as a witness.

"Ladies and gentlemen, this meeting is held to piece together the chain of events leading to this day. It's important that we leave no stone unturned. The ultimate goal is to show Mark Reeves' mysterious clients that this project is dead, their money wasted. Unfortunately, we haven't been able to pin any wrongdoing on Mark Reeves, except negligence. You can imagine how serious this is. People will be blaming Mark Reeves for everything. The public outcry will be immense."

"There are several financial transactions involving BIOGENCORP and the account with the name of Samuel Berry. We haven't been able to trace the account to any person, country, or company. Suffice it to say, we have no idea who first orchestrated the whole ordeal. However they are, commissioned BIGENCORP to create a new kind of weapon in light of the new international treaty banning nuclear weapons. Although, if someone goes out of his or her way to stay hidden, then it probably would have been more logical to actually create nuclear weaponry. Whatever the secret to creating these soldiers is, I doubt that Patrick Sandlak was the only one to know it. Thankfully, since the Pentagon isn't involved, there's no chance they will claim our friend here as their property."

Property? Arex wasn't comfortable about being thought of as some people's property. Not only that, but he felt like joining in the discussion, but found himself silent. What could he contribute, and hadn't Janiece told him to stay silent, and he had every intention not to let her down in such a formal setting, where his clothes and appearance made him stick out too much for his liking.

"Now, our initial suspicions arose when several transactions were being made to and from BIOGENCORP. The "to" we can't the origin of, but the from, we can establish the destination. The details are in he file. We also received an anonymous phone tip telling us that several scientists working for BIOGENCORP disappeared, all in one day. Who our anonymous tipster was, is unknown. Everyone we've interviewed insisted that it wasn't them. That tip gave me and my team enough cause to investigate. We were hoping to have had Mika infiltrate the company. She's had experience in forensic sciences. However, she did put us on the right track as she followed Patrick Sandlak around when he extradited Erickson Meyers from prison. Then, as everyone of us was trying to figure out what was going on, he transformed Erickson Meyers, much against his will."

Arex had to ask the question that was on his mind since the beginning.

"I still don't understand why I...or rather he, would accept to come with Patrick Sandlak with Janiece absent."

Arex regretted that statement. He didn't feel very comfortable in letting people know that he was unsure of his own identity. A lingering question in his mind was always: Was he Erickson Meyers, or someone else entirely?

"Actually, Meyers didn't really have a choice in the matter. He had to follow Sandlak, even though it probably meant... well...this. I'm sorry Arex," said Rodgers apologetically.

What followed was an awkward silence that loomed over everyone in the room. It felt heavy on Arex's shoulders like nothing else had. He felt the eyes looking at him, trying to gauge his reaction.

Afterwards, he stopped paying attention to what Rodgers was saying. He was distracted. Who was he? How could he function in this world? He would have to ask Corey Rodgers if he could recover the memories that were erased. He would then be able to live as Erickson Meyers once more. *Even if that means going to prison? Probably.*

"Let's leave things here until we have more information," said Rodgers. "Arex, can I have a word with you in private, please? The rest of you are dismissed."

Arex watched as everyone else left the conference room.

He was a little nervous about being alone with an influential individual like Rodgers. What did Rodgers think of him?

"Are you alright?"

Arex snapped out of his thoughts.

"I'm sorry. I have a lot on my mind."

"Like what?"

"For example, I feel heavy. I feel that my existence has caused such trouble. Certainly more trouble than I'm worth. I can imagine that everyone would be happier if I never came to be."

"And now you feel that we're stuck with you. I can imagine that that thought can distract anyone from practically everything. The news I have can only serve to make things worse, unfortunately."

"What is it?"

"We took a look at the Mind Shifter computer yesterday. We were hoping to be able to give you back the memories which were erased from your mind."

Arex perked up.

"It's great news. That means Jason can have his father back."

"No. It doesn't. BIOGENCORP's computers have a smart program that recognizes any attempt to hack them. The Mind Shifter saw that someone other than Patrick Sandlak was trying to access those memories and immediately erased them from its hard drive. Permanently."

That nearly destroyed Arex from the inside out. Now what? How was he going to tell Jason?

"What am I going to do now? Ever since I found out who I was, I couldn't wait to get those memories back. The bad the good...everything. I can't be Erickson Meyers anymore. Who can I be? How can I live like this?"

"It will be hard, but not impossible. You can live as Arex. We could give you a new name, a new identity."

Arex sat down. Rodgers didn't understand what he felt,

and what Jason felt even more. He looked at his hands. They weren't his. This body he was using, it belonged to a stranger. A stranger he would never know or meet, because he had effectively replaced him. That person was gone forever, and he was Jason's father, his only family. How could he live on knowing what his existence really meant to someone he cared about?

"It's... It's all my fault. Jason's father...he's gone, and there's nothing I can do to bring him back."

"Jason seems to accept you as a person."

"As a friend, maybe, but not as a father."

"Do you really want to be his father that much?"

"I would love to have a family. To not be alone. I feel like I'm alone, because of the way I look. There is no one else out there who can understand what I'm going through. I can't stand this. I'm not supposed to exist. Erickson Meyers should be the one here talking to you, not me."

"That's crazy talk. There was nothing you or Meyers could do to prevent this. If Meyers hadn't been erased, then we wouldn't have you. There would be a loss either way."

"But if I had never existed, none of this would have happened."

"You're right, none of this would have happened. Which also means that we wouldn't know about the A.R.EX. project until it was too late. Janiece would be dead, and Jason along with her, probably. Let me tell you one thing: You can't make an omelet without breaking eggs."

"Great. Jason's father is likened to food."

"Well, look at it this way: You won't have to deal with Meyers' criminal past, if it even exist. Officially, he is a convicted murderer. Unofficially, however, we are looking into the case file. Janiece has her suspicions about that particular case, and now that Kirk Hall is under investigation, every single one of his cases will be reviewed. This is also a big deal for us."

Arex felt no better about himself when he finally dragged his feet to the parking lot. Janiece asked him if he was okay, but he didn't answer. He was now afraid of saying anything at all. And now he had to explain everything he just heard to the both of them. Now what?

Chapter 2

Saturday, December 5th, 1998, 6:05 PM
Janiece Ryder's apartment

As the trial was fast approaching, the day came when Arex would speak to the public for the first time since he was discovered. Jason couldn't go, but Janiece told him he could watch everything live on TV. He wondered what kind of questions the reporters had for Arex.

The press conference was the news' top headline. Everyone around the world wanted to look at Arex and hear him talk.

Good evening ladies and gentlemen, the reporter announced, *Our top story tonight: The discovery of an anthropomorphic reptile existing among us. Last month, this being was first seen when it and a wounded F.B.I. agent arrived at Bellevue Hospital Center to be treated for various injuries. It was later revealed that another reptilian being committed suicide after having attacked them. The details in this matter are unknown. We now go live to the front of the F.B.I. New York City offices where the being will address the public for the first time.*

Jason saw Corey Rodgers stepping forward on the stand to give a short speech.:

"Thank you very much for coming here. As you already

know, Mr. Arex, who sits here on my right, isn't human. He is an anthropomorphic reptile who's agreed to testify in our favor in the case against BIOGENCORP, a private research facility based in Albany. He's also agreed to talk with you today and answer any questions you may have. Thank You."

Jason laughed as Arex walked up, shook Rodgers hand and then walked up to the stand. The camera then zoomed in on his father until half of his body showed. He shocked everyone in the crowd when he uttered the first few words.:

"Thank you, everyone, for coming here. As you know, my names is Arex and I'm not entirely human. I'm certain you have questions you would like to ask me, so, here I am. Please, raise your hands and I will pick one person at a time."

Jason chuckled. Every press conference was like that, but Arex didn't know that. All at once, everyone's hand seemed to shoot up. Arex looked around and finally pointed down at a man in a blue suit.

"My question is: What exactly are you?"

"That is not so easy to answer. As far as we know, I am the combination of the original human genome, with different species of reptiles. I don't know which ones, though."

The next question was just as strange.:

"Are you male?"

That drew more than a few chuckles out. Even Arex put his hand to his mouth, trying to keep a strait face.

"Yes. This is one question I can definitely answer. Yes I am male. Although, I can't understand why you're asking this."

Arex picked out another person in the crowd.

"Sir, if I may ask, is it true you have amnesia? Is it true that you used to be human? And if so, who were you?"

"I'm not sure if can answer that last part, but I was definitely human, although I don't remember being so. We've officially decided to refer to me as an entirely new person, since there is no way for me to recover the memories that were erased."

"We know BIOGENCORP was the reason you ended up like this. Are you going to sue them for what they've done?"

"It's not my place to judge them or bring them to court. Right now, I can't say that the entire company will face legal action. I have no idea how the legal system works. Well, I have a vague idea, but that's all."

"Is it true that you were created for, uh, less than legal reasons?"

What? What were they talking about? Was Arex really created to commit crimes?

"Yes. It's true. I was created with the purpose of killing people who obtained information about the project I was created in. It's ironic that I was the reason the F.B.I. is able to bring them to court."

Chapter 3

Thursday, January 7ᵗʰ, 1999, 10:37 AM
Albany County Courthouse, New York State

The evidence was stacked, the witnesses ready, and every base covered. It was now up to Janiece to win her first case as a lawyer representing the prosecution. There was a lot of pressure on her to succeed, but it was the kind of pressure she welcomed for once in her life. Now, it was her time to prove that she was the lawyer most everyone thought she ought to be. The defense, which was Mark reeves, ex-CEO of BIOGENCORP, was represented by Maxwell Shannon. Janiece had read his file, which included over fifty cases ranging in severity from domestic violence to white-collar corruption. Janiece knew she couldn't leave any stone unturned, because Shannon would surely take advantage of it.

As for Arex, the judge finally agreed to let him come wearing less than formal wear. Janiece could tell it was making Arex feel very uncomfortable, since he was even more visible now than he would have been in the cotton suit. Unfortunately, Arex seemed to have inherited Erickson Meyers allergy to cotton. Sometimes, Janiece pointed out, it was good to be a celebrity. She didn't tell Arex, but they and Jason would be having supper at an expensive restaurant which she reserved three weeks ago. She felt it was time for Arex to discover the outside world for a change.

It was likely Reeves knew the trouble he was in. Nevertheless, Maxwell Shannon entered a plea of "not guilty" on his behalf. Ever since Shannon came into the picture, Reeves stopped cooperating with the F.B.I.'s investigation, which was suspicious. She figured that Shannon liked to run the show on his own, which would probably present a conflict with his own client.

The two lawyers had just presented their opening arguments. Janiece now had witnesses to bring to the stand. The first to do so was Mika Nomura. Janiece told Arex to take notes on how people behaved in the stand, such as when they were sworn in.

"Mrs. Nomura, maybe you please explain to the jury your position."

"I am a special agent working for the F.B.I.. My superior is Corey Rodgers and he is the head the Criminal Investigation Division, or C.I.D. if you prefer, of the F.B.I.'s New York branch."

"Thank You. Now, please explain your involvement in the case at hand."

"Mr. Rodgers had sent me to work undercover as a forensic scientist at BIOGENCORP Laboratories. Unfortunately, all the positions were taken as Mr. Reeves told me. He did, however, promise me a position if I could offer my services temporarily as a signer."

"You are a certified signer, is that correct?"

"Yes. My late mother lost her hearing when I was very young. I learned sign language along with her so that we could communicate effectively."

"It seems strange that Mr. Reeves would need a signer in a laboratory."

"It wasn't an official position at BIOGENCORP. I was instructed to translate sign for Dr. Patrick Sandlak, so that he could understand Mr. Erickson Meyers, who was mute. Dr. Sandlak had with him a warrant to extradite Mr. Meyers from Bare Hill Correctional Facility, where he was serving his sentence for murder. Incidentally, the signatures on the extradition warrant were forged. That fact was confirmed by our experts."

"Why was my former client, Mr. Meyers, being extradited without my, or a judge's, legal consent?"

"Dr. Sandlak had offered Mr. Meyers compensation in exchange for volunteering to test a new experimental medicinal drug. The drug, Dr. Sandlak claimed, was able to regenerate human tissue, even tissue that was considered irreparably damaged."

"I gave Mr. Meyer specific instructions to communicate with me in matters such as this. Why wasn't I informed?"

"Dr. Sandlak told Mr. James Keith, the warden of Bare Hill, that you were unavailable."

"I am always available from my clients. I arrived there not two hours later with Jason Meyers, trying to find his father. I admit, your Honor, that I reacted to that news in an unbecoming way. No more questions, your Honor."

Maxwell Shannon rose up from the defendant's table and commenced his counter-interrogation.

"Let me start by asking this: Is it customary for prisoners to partake in testing an experimental drug?"

"It is uncommon, but not impossible. Usually, prisoners are called upon to perform custodial duties. In this case, it is my belief that Meyers, as other prisoners would later on, was chosen with the idea that no free man would ever volunteer for something like this."

"Everything was done in a legal manner, then?"

"No. Like I said, miss Ryder's signature was forged and so was the judge's. There is no doubt about that. If you're asking where my suspicions came from, it basically started when I asked Dr. Sandlak about the scars on his face. He lied and told me he was attacked by a Grizzly Bear. The scars were much too thin and straight to be caused by a wild animal that size."

"But all of this wouldn't be Dr. Sandlak's fault? How is my client in any way responsible?"

"Because he accepted forged document from Dr. Sandlak without looking into their authenticity."

After a short few seconds, Shannon declared.:

"No more questions, your Honor."

Chapter 4

Thursday, January 7ʰ, 1999, 6:45 PM
Manhattan District, New York City

Janiece felt Arex's surprise when they arrived at the *Royal Pallet* restaurant. He seemed even more surprised when he'd learned that she had reserved their seats three weeks earlier. He expressed his discomfort to her, but didn't back away from the idea of eating somewhere other than her apartment.

It wasn't as if Arex had a crude way of eating. It surprised her when she first saw him picking up a knife and fork and expertly cut through meat as if he'd done it for years. It was a positive thing for Arex to be left with Rick Meyers' skills, if not his memories. Janiece wondered if there was any skill Arex didn't retain. *Besides his lack of social bearings*, she thought.

They entered the restaurant, with everybody on the street and inside the place staring at them. It suddenly dawn on her that coming here with Arex was a risky decision. It would certainly spark rumors of them being a couple. It was crazy, how people can't resist a good tidbit.

"Reservations for Ryder," Janiece told the seating host.

"Yes, of course. We have been eagerly awaiting you," the host replied, but not without a glance to Arex and his casual clothing. Janiece rolled her eyes. It was good that Arex couldn't read the signs that said the host wasn't too pleased with letting someone in the eating area who didn't wear a suit.

When they sat down, there was an awkward silence. Everyone in the room had eyes only for them and that made Janiece feel a little self-conscious. She noticed that most people were giving them disdainful glances here and there as if trying not to seem interested in her and her celebrity client. There was even a rich-looking couple who left the room with half their plate still full.

Determined not to let everyone else's reaction get in the way of a good meal and experience, she asked for menus from one of the waiters. When they arrived, the three of them began looking at the food. After a couple of minutes, Arex asked.:

"Why are we eating here? I'm looking at these things and the prices they're selling them for and I can't believe anyone would pay for them. It's not like we can't eat these things at your house."

"It is expensive, but we're not just here for the food, you know. This is a great way to begin a social life."

"How?"

"There are people here. You never know who you might meet in places like this. I once meet an ex-boyfriend in a restaurant like this one. I know it's not logical, and it probably doesn't make sense to you, but being here, in public, is a good opportunity to meet other people. You have to be able to open up your mind to new experiences."

"I see. I just don't think I fit in in these settings. Everyone here is wearing formal clothing, and I'm not."

"Well, you're not a formal person. Besides, you are making the best first impression for yourself. Meeting someone goes both ways in mutual respect. Theses people also have to open themselves up to you. Remember, you're strange to them. They have to learn to accept you as we have."

"From what I've learned that's not going to be easy. I'm not just seeing these people stare at me, I'm feeling it as well."

"That can't be helped. Just try and put these stares aside and enjoy your meal. Maybe somebody will come and talk to you, maybe ask you a few questions."

"You mean personal questions. What if I don't want to answer them."

"Then answer another question. Remember: The secret to a good first impression is being open and having confidence in yourself. You have to trust yourself to say the right thing."

Their orders arrived. Everyone in the crowd seemed to stop eating and/or working just to look at the unlikely trio. Janiece had ordered Salmon with a Mediterranean salad on the side, while Arex chose a meal of Tortellini in Alfredo sauce, and Jason went with a filet mignon steak with mashed potatoes and peas on the side.

Right away, Janiece wasn't too sure about Jason being able, not only to finish the steak, but also keep it on his plate. Arex, on the other hand, was calm polite, and more mature than his mental age would suggest. Still, Janiece couldn't help but feel like he was holding something back from them. Something he might have been ashamed of. What could it be? Was it something she should be concerned about? How terrible a secret could that be?

"Janiece?"

Maybe he was going to open up now.

"Yes, Arex?"

"I have to tell you something. Well, to both of you."

"What is it?"

Jason was silent. He had stopped fiddling with his steak and was looking at them expectedly.

"Jason, do you remember when you told me that *Amazing Spider-Man* comic was your father's favorite? And that I told you I recognized it before I even knew what the story was between the pages?"

"Yeah."

"I know the answer to those questions now. You see, I first saw that comic book in a dream I had right before Janiece and I met. I saw this strange woman in a pink bathrobe, who told me she was disappointed in me, and that I was a monster for even thinking about...well, you know. It turns out that I'm what is left of your father, Jason. "

That hit Jason hard. His mouth went wide.

"You mean...you mean...how? That's...that's impossible... really?"

"Yes.

"Don't remember me?"

"No. I'm sorry. And I won't be able to remember anything before Halloween."

"Why not?"

"The computer that erased those memories had a failsafe that would permanently erase the data stored in it. Without those memories, I can't be your father. I'm sorry."

"Why didn't you tell us this?"

"I didn't know how to tell you. I was afraid you would blame me, that you would think I was trying to replace your father, but I'm not. You're not my son, you're my friend, the first friend I ever had and I wouldn't trade that, even for the chance to pretend that I'm someone I'm not. Your father's gone, Jason. I'm sorry. I can't even believe that I'm telling you this now...I have to go."

Before anybody could say anything to stop him, Arex stood up fast, and quickly walked out of the eating area, nearly ripped his jacket off the hanger in the hall, and left the restaurant while everyone else stopped what they were doing and stared.

* * *

Janiece watched as Arex left. He was humiliated by his own decision, that much was clear and the fact that he left ashamed by it meant he probably didn't want to face Jason's sadness or anger in the matter. Jason didn't seem too angry, but looked really sad.

"But he's my dad. Why did he say that he isn't."

"You have to understand, sweetie. He's went through a lot recently. Besides, as far he's concerned, he met you for the first time on Halloween morning."

"Why did he leave? Doesn't he like me?"

"Of course he does. He considers you his best friend."

"But why won't he be my dad?"

"Because he feels like he's your age. He's really a kid, just like you. He has enough on his plate right now. He will have to grow up a lot faster than you do because he's an adult. He feels the growing pains of dealing with dishonesty, suspicion on our part, fear, and death. You have to understand these feelings because you feel them too."

Jason nodded.

"You're right. He's still pretty cool, even if he's not my dad."

"I think so too. I also think he would make a great brother, what do you think?"

"Yeah."

With that, they also made their way out of the restaurant. They found Arex outside, beside the car, sitting on the stairs leading to a triplex. He was slumped on his right knee, with his left leg hanging slack on the steps. Janiece got Jason in the car, and then sat on the stairs next to him.

"What's on your mind?"

"I feel like I let everybody down. Jason's angry at me isn't he?"

"No. He thought that you didn't like him and that's why you claimed you weren't his father."

"That's not true. I'm just not Erickson Meyers, and I have

to accept that fact. I'm just sad because Jason has to accept it also. I just wish I could turn back the clock and prevent this entire mess from happening."

"If that were to happen, then you would never have existed, Jason's father would spend the rest of his life with the label of murderer, and Patrick Sandlak would still be alive, creating reptiles out of human beings. You have to realize that your existence is a blessing, not a curse, and you stop hurting over the negative side of what you represent. Understood?"

"I guess."

"No, there's no I guess. Promise me you'll stop brooding over this."

Arex looked up at her, then nodded

"I promise."

It was a solemn promise with a small grin attached to it. *Albeit half-hearted, it will have to do.*

Chapter 5

Another court day and this time Corey Rodgers was scheduled to testify. Janiece suspected that Maxwell Shannon took the time to dissect everything Mika Nomura had said just over a week ago. He probably had some detailed questions for Rodgers, especially seeing as he was Mika's superior.

"Mr. Rodgers," Janiece asked, "we have already heard from miss Nomura, one of the agents assigned to this case, that you are her supervisor and the head of C.I.D.. You assigned miss Nomura to this case. May you please explain how you came to the conclusion that you needed her to infiltrate the company."

"Yes ma'am. We had received an anonymous tip, warning us of corruption within BIOGENCORP's staff and administration. We were asked to look into their financial records, it was very vague. It's our duty to respond to any tip we receive, no matter how vague. In fact if the tip is anonymous, then there's something to be suspicious about."

"What did you find when acting on the tip?"

"We realized that BIOGENCORP was spending far too much money than needed to for the size of their roster and

160

the equipment they use. They spent that money on computer components. Every necessary individual computer component needed to create a computer from scratch."

"Surely not every single computer piece can be sold individually. I have BIOGENCORP's financial records in my hands. These components were ordered from various independent companies. How can these pieces not only fit together, but also allow for functioning and viable computers connected to an independent network?"

"It's a common misconception that technology varies from company to company. Just because a motherboard is made by a different company than the keyboard or the disk drive, doesn't mean all of these separate parts don't work together. A motherboard is a motherboard. They all have the same logic behind their build. A simple analogy is the video game market. A kid walks into a store, looking for a new controller for his PlayStation. He find several in stock, but the ones made by Sony might be a little too expensive for him. The kid will want to turn towards a cheaper alternative, and that's why stores carry accessories made by independent companies, because they cost less to carry on their shelves and they provide the consumer with inexpensive products. The same logic applies to this situation. C.E.O. Reeves chose the least expensive parts from different companies. Did it damper the performance he got from those computers? If anything, it made the computers run smoother and more powerful than a machine only using one brand of pieces."

"This would take an incredible amount of organization. How was it done? The defense and I have seen the floor plan of BIOGENCORP's building and nowhere was there any mention of a computer-creating laboratory as far as I know."

"As part of their expenses, they've been able to set up a subsidiary called NETREK. They made the computer's, their instruction manuals, and they installed them."

"Well that explains a lot, thank you. Now, during your

search of BIOGENCORP's building you were able to acquire these computers. Was there any evidence relevant to this case that was found on these computers?"

"Actually, we weren't able to find any information at all from these computers. Every one of BIOGENCORP's computers had a failsafe program installed into it. Any person who wasn't part of the company's staff who tried to access the files would see the hard drives erase itself before their very eyes. Nothing, not even the default programs, would be available. Unfortunately, that's what happened with our attempts. Every single computer's hard drive got erased. All their, data, all their logs, any information pertaining to the company, even their legitimate research is gone. It's almost as if the company never existed."

"I see. Thank you Mr. Rodgers. No more questions, your honor."

Maxwell Shannon started his counter-interrogation.

"You claim that you found a computer known as the Mind Shifter in the building. Tell me, how did you even find out about it?"

"One of BIOGENCORP's employees at the time stumbled upon the A.R.EX. file on the computers while she was defragmenting the hard disks on all computers."

"Yes, I am well aware of Daisy Carter. I am also aware that she wasn't on the roster for the A.R.EX. project. Why is it that she would make a copy of the file, when she wasn't even supposed to know what the project was? Not only that, but wasn't what she did known as stealing classified information?"

"To answer your first question, there is the human natural reflex for gossip. She could have heard about the project from any one of her colleagues. Second, yes, was she did could be called stealing. However, even if she stole classified information from her employers, she did not deserve to die because of that action."

"Nonetheless," Shannon interrupted, "she was in possession of information that she wasn't supposed to have. No district attorney would be caught dead issuing a warrant based on stolen information."

"Maybe not, but if a convicted criminal gets illegally extradited, then dies in the custody of an entire company, then there is cause for a warrant to search the premises."

"There is still the matter of my client's involvement in the case."

"Your client was the C.E.O. of BIOGENCORP, taking care of every administrative decision for the company. He allowed the purchase of these custom-built computers. He let Patrick Sandlak control his company, he accepted untold amounts of money from an unknown source he thought he could trust. He lead his employees in the creation of a project involving mass murder, and he never questioned the reasons motivating his sponsors. He was relaxing in the Bahamas while his employee's creation was sent to kill an innocent person for the wrong reason. He was enjoying ignorant bliss while one of his employees was being murdered by his own subordinate. This is not the behavior of an administrator of a company. This is why he is now facing charges."

* * *

That evening,
Janiece Ryder's apartment

There were many things bothering Arex as they ate supper that night. There was an anxious feeling that he couldn't really describe. It was possible he felt a twinge of regret for

Mark Reeves? Why was he being blamed for what Patrick Sandlak had done?

"I don't' understand, Janiece. Why is Reeves facing charges? He never did anything, did he?"

"That's exactly why he's being prosecuted," Janiece replied. "He's being prosecuted because he never did anything to stop Sandlak from creating you, sending you to kill me, turning himself into a reptile, murdering Daisy, and then trying to kill us all in a desperate attempt to avoid the dismantling of his project."

"But Sandlak did all these things. It's true, he did nothing to stop him, but neither did anybody else."

"You're right, and I'm sorry about that. It's just that neither me, nor the F.B.I. had anything that could stop Sandlak the legal way. I've told you before, when you're trying to built a legal case, you need proof."

"That much I understand, but that was in the past. Sandlak did awful things, but Reeves is the one paying the price. I don't think it's right."

"This is but one of the many negative sides of the American justice system. Sometimes, when corporate corruption is involved, the ignorant and the innocent also get caught up in a case they want no part of. Or they feel they've been treated unfairly. This is one of those cases. There is also pressure from the governments, the media, the public, who would want someone to be prosecuted, even if it might not be the right person."

"I don't want to be the one responsible for putting him in jail, when, according to my human genome, I should also be in prison."

"Again, you're right, but unfortunately, there's nothing we can do. The public will react negatively no matter what the jury's verdict is."

It became clear to Arex that justice wasn't a simple matter. He could only watch and see what would happen next.

Chapter 6

Friday, January 29ᵗʰ, 1999, 1:15 PM
Albany County Courthouse

There was a buzz of anticipation in the courtroom that day. The media wasn't allowed in the courtroom, yet every reporter outside the courthouse knew that Arex was to testify at last. Janiece wanted to leave both him and Mike Scatchard until the end, seeing as they were her more powerful witnesses. Besides, she wanted to let Arex see how a testimony was conducted.

Mike was the last piece of the F.B.I. puzzle. So far, everything was falling into place, and the defense couldn't seem to make a dent into the prosecution's case. It was, however, much too early to start thinking the case was won. There was only two witnesses left, and Janiece had to make sure they were as effective as she hoped.

"Mr. Scatchard, you are also an agent working for the F.B.I., is that correct?"

"Yes."

"And if my information is true, you have been frequently partnered with Mika Nomura ever since you began working there."

"That is true, ma'am."

"We've already heard the testimony from both your partner in the case and your superior. However, we don't quite have the whole picture painted for the audience and, especially, for the jury. May you please explain in detail what your role in this case was?"

"Certainly. Mr. Rodgers, our superior had become suspicious after his initial findings of BIOGENCORP's financial records. While Mrs. Nomura was working undercover, I discovered that some of their scientists had disappeared. All of them, all ten of them, disappeared on the same day, which was extremely suspicious. "

"When did these disappearances occur?"

"In July."

"Are they relevant to this case?"

"We've interrogated several employees and found out that all of them were likely working on the A.R.EX. project. We speculate that an experiment related to the A.R.EX. project might have ended in a disaster that caused the death of these scientists. This incident was quickly covered up, so this is pure speculation, but it would explain these disappearances and their cause. There is also proof in the financial records. Immediately after the speculated incident, there were payments made to BIOGENCORP from their anonymous sponsors and orders were made just as quickly for new computer components."

"One would think that if their employees were killed or crippled in an incident, that the families of these people would be told what happened. Maybe the company would help pay for the funerals or the medical bills. Am I wrong to think that that's what anyone with an ounce of common sense and perhaps even a hint of a guilty conscience would do. Have they done that?"

"No. The bodies of the scientists were found dumped across Highway 87. We suspect that their sponsors had a hand in that."

"I see. Thank you, Mr. Scatchard. No more questions, your Honor."

For once, Maxwell Shannon had no counter-interrogation for her witness. Janiece knew, by then, that the crowd was on her side, and possibly the jury, too. All she had to do now was let Arex tell his side of the story. She was confident at this point that she could pull off the win and show everyone she could be a great attorney.

"Your Honor," she called, "I would like to call Mr. Arex to the stand."

Just like that, the crowd was abuzz with whispers of anticipation. There was a strange feeling surrounding Arex as he stood up and proceeded to the stand. The officer with the bible stepped toward him, reaching the book out with his arm. Arex placed his right hand on the bible and put his left hand up as he saw every other witness do.

"Do you swear to tell the truth, the whole truth, and nothing but the truth?"

"I swear."

Janiece was certain that nobody who had ever taken the stand had such a captivated audience. Even judge Simmons couldn't help but lean over and take a closer look at the talking reptile wearing clothes.

"Mr. Arex, I would like to know how you came to be. We gave you the information we received during the investigation, but we would to go back, to when you first woke up. Forget about everything that happened from the time we met. I would like to know your perspective on things beforehand., so please, explain the events beginning on the early morning of October 29th."

"I first woke up on that morning and found myself in the middle of a bedroom. I didn't know why I was there, or how I got to be there. Patrick Sandlak was in the room with me. He asked me whether or not I knew anything about my whereabouts."

"Didn't he ask you whether or not you felt alright?"

"No."

"And what happened afterwards?"

"He told me that he had created me for the purpose of serving the American military. I was tested both physically and mentally. I found myself in an abandoned apartment in New York City on the afternoon of the 31st. I was told I was going to perform my first mission."

"You had just been created two days earlier. What purpose could it possibly serve to have you in New York City so soon after you had just woken up. Erickson Meyers has no military record, so you couldn't possibly have inherited any military knowledge from him. What on Earth could have made Dr. Sandlak think that you were combat or mission-ready?"

"Oddly enough, that didn't cross my mind."

"Alright. Next question: What were you supposed to do. What was the "American military" expecting you to do?"

"I was told that I had to...how can I say this...eliminate you."

Several people gasped at this new information. Whispers erupted all around the courtroom as the weight of Arex's words fell on everyone in the room. *There goes one bombshell,* thought Janiece as Judge Simmons had to call for order as people in the audience started talking, and the voices had gotten louder. Janiece decided it was best to continue and let the masses know everything.

"Why would Dr. Sandlak want me dead?"

"All I knew at that point was from a file folder he gave me. It described you as a ruthless defense attorney with ties to organized crime. It also said that you weren't above killing in order to stop key witnesses from testifying against your clients."

Dr. Sandlak had obviously not thought about looking into my records as a lawyer, she wanted to say, but held her tongue.

"Alright then, we can all see that I'm still alive, so it seems pretty obvious that you didn't quite take what was in that folder to heart. What did make you decide not to kill me?"

Janiece felt the audiences eyes bearing down on them. This was a crucial point in the trial. Arex was about to describe his motivations behind that life-changing decision that had brought them all here to this day.

"I had arrived at the apartment with every intention of killing you. I really thought that that was what I needed to do, because it was necessary to stop you from committing criminal acts. As I thought more and more about it, however, it dawned on me that this "mission" I had been given was suspicious. Why would the military, which I knew was supposed to focus its efforts on going to war with hundreds of soldiers at a time against hundreds of other soldiers from somewhere else, focus any kind of resources on one person, no matter how bad that person was? I had the sneaking suspicion that there had to be an authoritarian organization that was better suited to deal with a rogue lawyer. As it turned out, my thoughts were correct, because we have the people like the officers of the New York City Police Department and the Federal Bureau of Investigation, and they have the authority on these matters, not the military personnel."

"And that's what gave you your first suspicions. Is there anything else that gave you pause, and had you thinking: "maybe this isn't such a good idea"?"

"A nightmare I had. Whenever I would imagine even hurting you, I'd feel terrible. And then, there was strange dream I had where I had actually succeeded in killing you, but then there was this voice. I turned around, and I found myself in this void. There was a woman there and she held a comic book in her hand."

"Wait, did I heard this right? Did you say you saw a woman holding a comic book in her hands?"

"As strange as it sounds, yes. She was really angry at me,

telling me how I broke a promise, that I became a monster. I couldn't understand, because I didn't know who she was and why she was saying these things about me. Before I knew it, she disappeared, and I woke up."

"You've never told me this before."

"That's because even I didn't believe it. I thought it was all my imagination, or my conscience trying to speak to me. I was able to piece everything together when I was told that I had Erickson Meyers' DNA. It turns out that the comic book the woman was holding was his favorite, according to Jason that is."

Janiece started to regret having put Arex on the stand. He had just blurted out a story she'd never heard before. Not only that, but it gave Maxwell Shannon something to latch on to and twist into something that put his client in a better light. Shannon had already gotten up and stood in front of the stand. He had a bit of a smile on his face.

"Tell me, Mr. Arex, you saw my client the day that the F.B.I. searched BIOGENCORP's building. Had you ever seen him before that day?"

"No."

"And yet you single they clearly singled him out to you."

"Miss Nomura had pointed him out to me and asked me whether or not I recognized him. I told both her and Mr. Rodgers that I didn't. This is the truth, I had never seen him before. Until then, I thought Patrick Sandlak was in charge of the entire company."

"Do you think my client deserves to pay for Dr. Sandlak's crimes."

"No, I don't. Not as far as I know."

"You don't seem too sure of yourself."

"I don't know Mr. Reeves. I can't judge him only based on what I've heard of him."

"Nice sentiment. That's the way everything should be.

And I suppose it would be too much too ask of you to tell me what you think of him."

"Yes."

Then, Janiece watched as the counter-interrogation took a strange turn.

"And what about you? What about your situation as a person?"

"I beg your pardon?"

"What I mean is this: we all known you currently live with miss Ryder and Jason Meyers. Using this logic, would it be wrong for anybody to assume that you have a connection with these people, and subsequently Erikson Meyers?"

"Yes, I have a connection with miss Ryder. As for Jason, he's a good friend."

"Do you consider him only a friend?"

"Yes. Why are you asking this?"

"It seems strange that you would consider someone who is essentially your flesh and blood "only a friend". Technically, you did help give birth to him."

"But it wasn't me, it was Rick Meyers. He was Jason's father. I'm not."

"I can't believe that you would say this right in front of him. Who wouldn't want to claim fatherhood to such a fine young boy?"

"Who said that I didn't want to? What if I did claim I was his father? You would be here telling me that I wasn't, that I was trying to pretend to be someone I'm not."

"And yet you would think that Jason would be emotionally distressed at the thought of living with someone who used to be his father, and who doesn't consider himself to be that person."

"You can't be serious. Jason's emotions are his business. Not mine, not yours, his. If he is emotionally distressed, it's not your job to emphasize it. You can't take advantage of a child's feelings, not matter what they are."

"I am not trying to take advantage of anybody. You, on the other hand, have succeeded in getting yourself out of jail using amnesia and a new body as an excuse."

"Objection, your honor," Janiece intervened, "Mr. Shannon is trying to imply that my client is the one who is on trial and not his."

"Sustained. Mr. Shannon, you will refrain from making accusations against the witness on the stand without any proof."

"Your Honor."

Everyone turned to see Arex, who had stood up from the seat. Judge Simmons was mildly surprised.

"Yes, Mr. Arex?"

"I know that it might not be my place to ask this, but I don't want to answer Mr. Shannon's questions any more. None of them had anything to do with the case so far. For some reason, he tried to make me feel guilty for having put his client on trial. When that didn't work, he went after my relationship with Jason, which is none of his business. It doesn't make sense and, quite frankly, I didn't want to have any part of this trial to begin with."

"You didn't? Why are you here, then?"

"My intention was to bring Patrick Sandlak to justice. That was also the intention on the part of the F.B.I. agents and miss Ryder. When that didn't work out as planned, everyone else decided to go after Mr. Reeves, and I just couldn't understand why.   Now I understand. People want people to be punished for a crime committed. Sometimes what happens is that people lose sight of what is truly important and just want revenge, no matter whose life is ruined in the process. These people are made up to be examples or become martyrs. I should know, because I became a martyr, a poster boy for a crazy project created by an angry person who couldn't understand why people die needlessly. Do I forgive Patrick Sandlak for what he did to me? I can't, because he died and now his employer is paying the price for what he did. He left the world a coward, and he left people with the desire for revenge."

"This isn't about revenge. This is about justice for what happened and what could have happened," said Janiece.

"You don't really believe that anymore. Do you really think it necessary to have Mr. Reeves in jail? With Patrick Sandlak dead, the A.R.EX. project will no longer be a viable idea. Don't you think that justice has been done already?"

Janiece had swallowed a bitter pill just now. He was right. She had put her ideals aside in an effort to win her first case as a prosecution lawyer.

"Well Mr. Arex, what would you recommend? I'm asking you this because you seem to have more common sense than everyone else here."

"I don't want Mr. Reeves to pay for Sandlak's crimes. They were and are two different people. After all, you've all been using the same logic with me."

Out of the corner of her eye, Janiece saw Reeves eyes stare straight into Arex. It was unclear what he was thinking, but she figured he was thanking his lucky stars.

"Done," said the judge, "Mr. Reeves, it seems you have just been acquitted. You are free to go."

When he said that, the entire courtroom seemed to come alive. Arex, on the other hand, was dumbfounded.

"Really? You're letting him go just because I didn't want him to go to jail?"

"Yes, Mr. Arex. After all, this entire trial was put together on the basis that you were the plaintiff against Mark Reeves for criminal negligence. Your plight was the lynchpin of this case. You've basically told us that you were dropping all charges. Unless, of course, I'm mistaken."

"No, you're not. I really am dropping all charges."

With that, the case was said and done. Since the charges against Mark Reeves were dropped, he was a free man. He was extremely emotional when he answered the media's questions surrounded by his family. The F.B.I. and Janiece decided it was best to accept Arex's decision, but weren't content until Reeves promised to pay for the compensation Patrick Sandlak had promised Erickson Meyers before extraditing him. Janiece was still a little peeved, and was prepared to let Arex know about it

Chapter 7

Friday, January 29th, 5:34 PM
Janiece Ryder's apartment

Arex knew that Janiece was mad at him for having stopped the trial, but he never expected her to have exploded the way she did.

"I can't believe you did that! How could you? You let Reeves go, even though he had just as much to do with the A.R.EX. project as Sandlak did."

"Yes. He had just as much to do with the project. The project as it was originally intended."

"And what is that supposed to mean?"

"It means that the project was intended as a legitimate idea to create a military weapon. Think about it: Did Reeves have any idea who had really hired him? What exactly is evil, Patrick Sandlak or the project he used to try and cover up his actions?"

"What about the person who put him in a position of power? Reeves should have known what his friend was going to do. His friend, Arex."

"I'm your friend, aren't I? That didn't stop you from using me. I thought the whole idea behind the trial was justice, not revenge. Ad I also thought that you had your priorities straight, but maybe I was wrong. I didn't like the fact that you started the trial in my name without telling me."

* * *

Janiece was still angry, but slowly, that anger was turning against herself. She wanted to tell Arex off, but he ended up telling her off. She felt his anger and was a little afraid of him.

"I'm sorry. I should have told you these things. The truth is, I felt like I had something to prove, not just to the world, but to myself. I first became an attorney with the idea that I wanted justice for those accused of various crimes. I felt like it was my job to speak for these people and to actually care for them and about them. That's why I wanted to adopt Jason. I cared about Jason and I felt that the case was my responsibility. As time went on, I guess I got frustrated with constantly being disrespected because I kept choosing to help the defendant in a case, and rarely winning a case. I was beginning to think that my career had taken a wrong turn and hit a dead end."

"Why didn't you tell us any of this? Janiece, why can't you trust me?"

"You're not an easy person to trust. How can I trust you, now? You went over my head and stooped the trial. Reeves gets away with..."

"With what? Losing his job? Being humiliated in public? Seeing the possibility of losing his freedom because of what someone else did? I suppose that means he wasn't being punished enough. Truly he deserved to lose his freedom, his family, after having already lost a lot of money."

"He was inattentive as to what was going on right under his nose, and then he left control of his company to a power-hungry maniac who took a life and ended it."

"So this is about revenge. You feel that Sandlak hurt you

by taking Jason's father, destroying him and creating me in the process. Instead of being able to bring Sandlak to justice, you placed the blame on his employer. I know that I'm a little inexperienced when it comes to life, but I know this much: it's wrong to take somebody, blame him for crimes committed by someone else, and basically destroy his life. How is Mark Reeves going to live his life now? I don't care what happened to me. I don't remember being anybody other than who I am now, so let it go."

Janiece did let it go. It was no use arguing with him since he had a point. It just irritated her to know that he was the very ideal of kindness. She gave him a warm smile and drew a deep breath.

"I hate it when you're so nice. But you're right, and I was wrong. And I'm tired of fighting you."

DING-DONG!

Janiece sighed. It was a very emotional moment and it was officially ruined.

"I'll get it."

She opened the door to the pair of Mike and Mika, the two F.B.I. agents. They wore some thin smiles.

"We heard your tirade all the way at the end of the hall," said Mike, "so we figured we'd wait until you lovebirds had calmed down. We came here with some name suggestions for Arex to start his new life with. Also, Mark Reeves was so thankful that the charges were dropped that he added another million to the compensation payment. Arex, your practically set for life."

Mike gave Arex a sheet of paper.

"Uh...thanks. I'd still prefer it if I got a job, though."

"That won't be a problem," said Mika. "I'll bet there'd be plenty of people who would want to hire you. The question is: where will you live?"

Arex thought the question over. He turned to Janiece and asked:

"I don't suppose you'd tolerate for another few days until I find a place to live?"

Everybody in the room broke into laughter.

"No. The honor is all mine, Mr....?"

Arex looked at the sheet Mike gave to him.

"Alex. Alex Rivers. That's my name."

Epilogue

Six months later,
New York City

Days went on. As quickly as fall turned into winter, winter, in turn, melted into spring. It was a whirlwind at first, but life had finally begun to settled down for Arex. Though he got a new name for himself, it wasn't easy for anyone to call him by such a generic name as Alex.

His life was beginning to shape up pretty nicely. He apprenticed for a while and got a job working for a construction company and was obtaining his necessary elementary and later high school diplomas through correspondence courses. He was also working on getting his own black belt in Aikido, which he had become fond of practicing.

As for Janiece and Jason, change hadn't come too easily, but he insisted on repaying their kindness and hospitality with a portion of his salary. The three of them had formed a lasting bond, and he knew he would always be welcome at their apartment. Jason had come to think of him as an older brother more than a father figure, which suited Arex just fine all things considered, since he quickly found that that he was too lenient toward Jason to be an effective parent. His feelings for Janiece were never fully admitted to, but romance wasn't exactly on a lawyer's agenda. He felt somewhat comfortable knowing that the two of them would remain friends.

For now, though, he was busy settling into his new apartment. He had rented an apartment a few blocks from Janiece's building. He actually couldn't even move in right away because of the smell. The apartment had previously been rented by an old woman who had three cats. He had taken upon himself to clean, redecorate, and get rid of just about everything there, and have everything new. He was told that it was somewhat of a tradition for someone moving into a new home to hold a housewarming party. Janiece, Jason, Joe Henry, and the F.B.I. pairing of Mika Nomura and Mike Scatchard were all present and huddled up in his living room. Even Mark Reeves, whom many in the room disapproved of, was enjoying Arex's hospitality.

Arex felt a twinge of pride after having prepared all of the food himself. Cooking was quickly becoming one of his favorite hobbies. He discovered a talent for preparing foods that everyone enjoyed, if he judged well by the emptying plates across his kitchen counter.

For the occasion, he also wanted to unveil a special banner that he had been preparing for a while. Gathering everyone around, he finally took the veil off and revealed what was going to be his rules of conduct in life:

Life Rules

1. *I am not a violent person, nor am I a thief or a murderer.*
2. *I shall never be haunted by the ghosts of my past or the circumstances surrounding my creation.*
3. *I will never agree with what other people say about me unless what they say suits my perception of myself.*
4. *I will life my life the way I choose to live it, and*

not the way preconceptions or outside influences dictate it to be.

5. *I will always strive to find a balance between selfishness and selflessness.*
6. *I will always be proud of being unique in this world.*
7. *I will never be thought of as anything less than a person.*
8. *I am proud of who I am, and that is Alex Rivers. Arex.*

The End